Cruising With Danger

by

Robyn Rychards

Louisiana Heat Series

Cruising With Danger

Cover Art by *Diana Carlile*

The Wild Rose Press, Inc.
PO Box 708
Adams Basin, NY 14410-0708
Visit us at www.thewildrosepress.com

Publishing History
First Crimson Rose Edition, 2018
Print ISBN 978-1-5092-2057-1
Digital ISBN 978-1-5092-2058-8

Louisiana Heat Series
Published in the United States of America

As her blood heated,

Sage resisted the urge to fan herself. *Detective* Langdon? She'd done more than her share of detective work with members of the Chicago police force, but it wasn't of the criminal variety. *Investigating* this particular officer held more appeal than all those other cops combined. Which only made her want to run screaming from the room in self-preservation.

Instead, she focused on the shiny buttons of Captain Southerby's uniform and concentrated on his words. "Keep me in the loop about what you discover, Detective, but leave me out of the day to day things. Sage, it goes without saying that as far as the rest of the crew is concerned, other than the Chief of Security, Mr. Langdon is simply one of our new security guards."

She couldn't help it, she looked at Caribbean Seas' newest security guard again. Then he looked at her, snaring her with the heated gaze of those unusual eyes.

And his words. *Good God*, his words. "I'm looking forward to…*working* with you, Dr. Brady."

Dedication

To my best friend, Celeste.
Thanks for always being there.

Acknowledgments

Special thanks to Jan Meredith for all your help brainstorming this story, as well as sharing your knowledge of all things medical as an ER nurse.

Thanks to Dr. Hans Elzinga for sharing your medical expertise.

Shout out to Amalie Berlin for your encouragement to tackle a medical romance.

Thanks, Incy Black, for your support and encouragement.

Chapter One

He was Sage Brady's kind of man. Dark and rugged, with an aura of danger and a curious magnetic pull that wasn't pretty-boy handsome but had every female in his orbit wanting to stay there.

The man sat across from the captain, who was at his teak desk, and watched Sage as she entered the spacious office. Well, spacious compared to her office anyway. It was a cruise ship, after all. His expression made her pause on the threshold. Dark brows pulled together over the palest blue eyes she'd ever seen and took him from intriguingly dangerous to intimidating. The guy emanated some serious back-off vibes, yet it didn't stop her from marveling at the color of his eyes. Or admiring his heart-stopping physique and over-long dark hair the color of warm maple syrup. Who was he and what was he doing here? This was supposed to be a private meeting with the captain to go over her new position.

She gave the man another quick look as she quietly closed the door behind her and crossed the room. A bad feeling landed in her stomach and her intuition was rarely wrong. It's what had made her a successful ER doctor. But she certainly didn't need to be thinking about her past right now. Or him. She was no longer *that* Sage Brady, stressed out and desperate to prove something to her father.

She was grateful when the captain interrupted her thoughts, and drew her attention away from the first man to threaten her peace of mind since she left her old life behind.

"Dr. Brady, please take a seat."

"Of course, sir. I'm not too early, am I?"

"No. Punctual as usual," Captain Southerby murmured. "One of the many reasons why I chose you to temporarily take over Dr. Roberts' position as Chief Medical Officer. It's been a while since we worked together, so I'm looking forward to working with you again on the *Caribbean Sunrise*."

As she made her way across the room, Sage looked at the stranger one more time. She hadn't noticed he wore a security guard's uniform. Maybe because the initial impression the man gave was one of authority. She sank into the chair, wishing it was across the room from him rather than mere inches away, and gave him another quick glance. *Security guard, my ass.* She put the brakes on that line of thought. Not her circus, not her monkeys.

Still, why was a security guard here?

She forced herself to focus on Captain Southerby who looked as immaculate as always. Neatly trimmed gray beard, hat at just the right angle on his bald head, uniform perfectly arranged. His appearance as in control as he was of the ship. As he ran a hand over his goatee she noted his brown eyes didn't carry their usual twinkle. Her stomach flipped. She'd rarely seen him without that little dance in his eyes.

"First of all, Dr. Brady, I want to thank you for stepping in. I know you're more than capable of handling the job."

"Thanks for the vote of confidence. I'm determined to prove your faith isn't misplaced."

It was an effort not to fidget. This may very well be her circus. *Damn it*. She was so over being part of a circus. That's why she was a doctor on a cruise ship now, not in an emergency room. She braced herself for whatever might come next. Like the fact she was now interim Chief Medical Officer because her friend and mentor, Dr. Eric Roberts was dead wasn't bad enough?

"Forgive my bad manners, Doctor, for not introducing you to Dace Langdon, our new hire. Dace, this is the woman I was telling you about, Sage Brady. She's been with the line for about three years now."

Captain Southerby ran a hand over his goatee again and gave his head a slight shake. Her heart rate picked up and she surreptitiously wiped her hands on her skirt. Before either of them could look at each other in acknowledgment of the introduction, the captain continued.

"Sage, forgive me for being blunt." His eyes flicked to Dace Langdon. "Mr. Langdon has informed me that Dr. Roberts' death wasn't from natural causes. He was murdered."

She felt the color drain from her face and blurted out the first thought that came to mind, regardless of tone or professional courtesy. "Forgive *me*, Captain, but why the hell is a security guard the one to inform you of this fact? I thought Eric died of a heart attack, which is a natural cause."

She looked at Dace Langdon and didn't bother to hide her suspicion. When her gaze collided with his icy blue one, she had the sensation of a fast downhill ride on a roller coaster.

"I'm sorry for your loss, Dr. Brady."

"Thank you, Mr. Langdon. I didn't mean to be rude, but this is as much of a shock as when I learned my friend was dead."

Expression momentarily sympathetic, he nodded. "Maybe you should take a deep breath and give the captain a moment to explain."

All she could do was nod for fear her voice would betray her. He didn't need to know his voice, with its hint of roughness and trace of a southern accent, had her insides turning to mush. It certainly didn't help when he raised a hand toward her in a gesture of comfort and her skin tingled in anticipation of his touch.

She grabbed desperately for her usual emotional distance, a necessary part of being a physician who didn't always have good news to deliver and forced herself to focus on Captain Southerby.

"For your ears only, Dr. Brady," he said. "You haven't been assigned to work on the same ship as Eric Roberts for quite a while and weren't part of his staff when this happened. Mr. Langdon is a police officer, joining our cruise on assignment. He'll be acting as a security guard, which will allow him the access he needs to find out what he can about Dr. Roberts' death without alerting anyone who may have been involved. It's also less of a disruption to our passengers' enjoyment of their cruise if they see him as one of the many security guards on board."

The captain looked at Dace Langdon, which only drew her attention to the man all over again. It would be easier to pretend he wasn't there because when he spoke she imagined his voice saying things that could never be said in front of her boss. Scary, really, since the actual words were so far removed from what she imagined.

"Suspicious circumstances called for an autopsy on Roberts," he said in a slow, dark way that made Eric and his autopsy the last thing she was thinking about. "The results came back yesterday."

Impatient, and wanting to be a million miles away, she fought the urge to squirm in her seat. "And the results are?"

"He was injected with a poison which made it appear he died of a heart attack."

Folding his hands, the captain leaned forward, his expression serious. Sage no longer felt the urge to wiggle. "So, Dr. Brady, Detective Langdon will need information from you about the medical staff. Since you've been the staff doctor for the Caribbean Seas Cruise Lines up until now, I'm sure you'll be able to provide helpful information."

Translation: spy on her coworkers. Now she was irritated. It would've been nice to know that was in the job description before she accepted the position. "What kind of information?"

"To start, he needs a list of everyone Dr. Roberts worked with during his last assignment on board this ship. Since you're not a suspect, I want you to help him with whatever he requires, so I can focus on running this ship."

As her blood heated, Sage resisted the urge to fan herself. *Detective* Langdon? She'd done more than her share of detective work with members of the Chicago police force, but it wasn't of the criminal variety. Investigating this particular officer held more appeal than all those other cops combined. Which only made her want to run screaming from the room in self-preservation.

Instead, she focused on the shiny buttons of the captain's uniform and concentrated on his words. "Keep me in the loop about what you discover, Detective, but leave me out of the day to day things. Sage, it goes without saying that as far as the rest of the crew is concerned, other than the Chief of Security, Mr. Langdon is simply one of our new security guards."

She couldn't help it, she looked at Caribbean Seas' newest security guard again. Then he looked at her, snaring her with the heated gaze of those unusual eyes.

And his words. *Good God*, his words. "I'm looking forward to…*working* with you, Dr. Brady."

She fought the old Sage Brady battling to get out of the box she shoved her into when she'd packed up and moved to New Orleans. Helping the sexiest police detective she'd ever run across with a murder investigation was the kind of thing the old Sage thrived on.

New and improved Sage was seriously screwed.

****

Shit.

Was he feverish? Had those words really come out of his mouth? In front of the *captain*? Why couldn't Dr. Brady be some old pill pusher, finishing out his career on a cruise ship? What was a gorgeous creature like Sage Brady doing working as a doctor for Caribbean Seas?

Maybe she wasn't good enough to work anywhere else. Maybe the captain put her in charge because he had no other option. For all Dace knew, it was her looks that got her the job in the first place. Chief Medical Officer was a big accomplishment for anyone at her age. A motive for murder, too. But the NOPD had thoroughly checked her out before bringing her on board with the investigation. No need to even go there.

Her dark hair had some sort of shaggy cut that barely reached her shoulders and had no right to look so stunning. It should make her look unkempt. The fact it didn't was irritating. Hell, it made her look like she'd just rolled out of bed after a long night of…

Don't even think it, Langdon. But geez, her luscious curves had him thinking the same thing. Of course, the way she wore a boring ship doctor's uniform didn't help. No one should be allowed to look so good in something so mundane. It was easy enough for him to mentally strip her of it, though. Down to her underwear, which, of course, had to be lacy, and black… He put a screeching halt on that train of thought. It didn't do him any good and it was seriously disrespectful.

"Do you need me for anything else, Captain? I have a lot to do before we leave New Orleans tomorrow."

"No. Go ahead and get back to work, Dr. Brady. Thanks for all your help."

"I'm happy to do whatever I can for Eric, you know that, Captain. Detective, if you need me, I'll be in the infirmary."

All Dace could do was nod. Mainly because the soothing tone in her voice made him forget all his troubles and left him wanting to listen to it for hours. He also couldn't take his eyes off her fine ass as she walked across the room and let herself out. *Damn it.*

For the first time in his adult life he forgot to open the door for a woman. Maybe it was a good thing since his fingers itched to grab that ass so staying in his seat kept temptation out of reach. He swiped a hand down his face and returned his attention to the captain.

Losing his focus is what landed him here, away from all the action, investigating a murder. Away from New Orleans where the murder took place. Captain Rocque gave him this assignment because Dace point-blank refused to take a vacation. Surely at some point things would start turning around for him. They better because this marked an all-time low in his career. Working with Dr. Brady would make things all the more challenging.

"Beautiful and smart, that one, Detective. Don't let her looks deceive you. She'll be an asset to your investigation."

"I hope you're right, Captain. Your help in this matter is greatly appreciated. I'll do my best not to interfere with the passengers' enjoyment of their cruise."

The captain nodded. "Eric Roberts was a friend as well as a colleague. If he was murdered by one of my crew, I'm as eager as you to catch the culprit."

"Rest easy, sir. We're covering every angle. Since he was killed in his home, the bulk of the investigation is focused on New Orleans. However, the murderer has enough medical knowledge to know about poisons which mimic a heart attack. It's necessary to investigate his medical team, though in this day and age all you need is access to the internet to research the method and means—as well as obtain the tools necessary to accomplish it. Odds are the medical crew wasn't involved but it's unwise to rule out anything right now."

"I hope you're right. However, I'm happy the New Orleans Police Department is doing everything they can to find the person who did this."

"We're on the same page then. Whatever it takes to get a murderer behind bars."

****

After closing the door to the captain's office, Sage leaned against the adjacent wall. She needed the support for her shaking legs—actually pretty much everything was shaking.

The captain had assigned her to assist a man who was the epitome of everything she admired in the male species. She had a weakness for members of the police force. And the fact that this was her first encounter with a detective in a very long time… She'd never felt so drawn to a man in her life and in a way that went beyond the physical.

Detectives were smart. And observant. The skills she needed to do her job well were the very same things she admired in others. Which complicated *everything*. She stiffened her spine.

You can do this. New and improved Sage was strong.

Eric was murdered. She could barely wrap her mind around the concept. The killer could very well be one of the medical crew. Wasn't that the purpose for having Detective Langdon on board? They were getting ready to embark on a five-day cruise through the Caribbean, which meant, whenever they weren't in port, they could be trapped on board with a cold-blooded killer.

Sage took a deep, calming breath in an attempt to keep her thoughts from heading down a crazy tangent because of the shocking information she'd received. Maybe Eric's death wasn't connected in any way to his life on board the ship. She certainly couldn't imagine anyone she worked with being capable of something so deliberate, so cold blooded. Medical professionals were in the business of helping people, not hurting them.

With a slight shake of her head and a slow count to ten, she felt her composure return. Pushing herself away from the wall, she headed toward the deck rather than her office. Some fresh air while she came to grips with everything was a better idea. She liked taking in the view of New Orleans from atop a cruise ship, which often seemed more like a floating hotel.

As she walked out into the sunshine and warm, muggy air of the south, her spirits lifted. Moving here from Chicago, away from the cold, away from the chaos her life had become, was a good decision. Hard as it had been to do at the time.

She stood at the railing, her back to the crew as they performed the routines of getting a ship ready to embark. Checking life boats, cleaning the deck in preparation for the passengers set to arrive tomorrow, making sure all the equipment was in working order. The sounds of their chatter and the splash of the water hardly registered as she tried to wrap her head around this latest development.

Her stomach did a little somersault; the skin on the back of her neck tingled in warning. Unfortunately not soon enough for her to realize the cause and react.

"I have a feeling Dr. Roberts was more than merely a colleague."

Dace Langdon's voice heightened the reaction his presence evoked. That hint of a southern drawl meant he most likely wasn't originally from the South, though it was more of an accent than she'd gained herself by living here. Probably because she didn't really spend much time in New Orleans, despite the fact she, and her friend and colleague Celeste, had shared an apartment there for a couple of years.

He braced his arms on the railing next to her while she forced herself to fix her gaze on the hustle and bustle of the crew restocking the ship with enough food and supplies for five days at sea. From this vantage point they reminded her of busy ants walking in a line, carrying their treasure into the ant pile, but the smell of the sea with its hint of fishiness permeating the air didn't quite fit in with that scenario.

In her peripheral vision she noticed him turn around to lean his hips against the railing, then cross his arms over his chest. A move which brought him close enough for his scent to swirl around her. Clean, woodsy, and altogether masculine, and much more pleasurable than the stale sea air of the port. She breathed it in deeply before she realized what she was doing. *God, he smelled good enough to make her forget every single resolve she made when she moved down here*. She didn't dare give in to the temptation to look at him.

"I'm not sure how relevant my relationship with Dr. Roberts is to your investigation, Detective, but yes. Did you follow me out here to ask me that? I thought I wasn't on your list of suspects."

"You're not, *chère*. I just wanted to offer my condolences and let you know it's not my intention to make a hard time more difficult. However, that doesn't change the fact I *will* be making things difficult, whether I intend to or not. We need to talk in private. *Now*."

"How did you find me? I said I'd be in the infirmary."

"Chance. I came out here to have a look."

She sighed and moved back from the railing, forcing herself to ignore the thrill his use of the endearment gave her. She'd been in New Orleans long enough to know calling someone *chère* meant nothing. Probably as little as the friendly look on his face and the warm smile he gave her, since it didn't match his tone of voice. The voice of a police officer ordering someone to cooperate or else. It took everything she had not to flinch when he ran his hand down her arm from shoulder to elbow and stepped closer.

She glared at his hand, then his face. "What the hell do you think you're doing?"

"My job. We're drawing attention to ourselves out here."

She took a quick peek over her shoulder. A couple people had paused what they were doing to watch them. Several others were close enough to hear what they were saying, even though they weren't looking at them.

"Do you think anyone heard me?"

"Most likely not, you were facing away from them, however, it's best if we speak in private. We can do it in my cabin, yours, or your office. Pick one."

He moved his hand from her elbow to her lower back and turned her toward the ship. Shock at his high-handedness had her moving along with him as he escorted her from the deck back inside, where she finally gathered her wits and came to a stand-still. "Who do you think you are? You can't just drag me to your cabin, or wherever, to talk. I don't care if you're a cop, no one manhandles me."

"Like I said, Dr. Brady, I'm doing my job. And if I remember correctly, your captain's orders were to cooperate. I need to speak with you behind a closed door. So, again, where would you like to go?"

She bit back an unprofessional word, starting to feel like accepting the job of Chief Medical Officer was the worst decision of her life. And she'd made some bad ones.

"My office."

He nodded and winked. "Though disappointing, probably the best choice."

Turning away from the enticing glitter in his eyes, she headed down the hall, hoping her fast pace would leave him trailing behind. To her chagrin he matched her stride for stride, staying at her side the entire way and held the door of the infirmary open for her, a courtesy she hadn't expected. When he placed his hand in the small of her back, she bit back a growl of frustration. There were several staff members in the waiting area, and she didn't want to cause a scene by telling him to keep his hands to himself.

His hand remained firmly in place as they made their way to her office. Since they passed several people on the way she couldn't do anything more than avoid eye contact and walk as quickly as possible. What in the world would everyone think now? Why was he acting like he had a right to be so personal? She hadn't been seen in such close proximity with a man since she started working for Caribbean Seas. So much so, it wouldn't surprise her if the crew started wondering if this one was special.

He was special all right, but not that kind of special. Especially arrogant, more like. She bit back a sigh. She knew what arrogant looked like and it wasn't this man. Her father, on the other hand... And she thought she was past letting father issues affect her.

As he closed her office door behind them, she hurried to her desk. It was a little heart-wrenching to now have Eric's office, but it was nice to have one that was roomier than the one her previous position allotted. Though not as large or as neat as the captain's, she was grateful for the space—and a large object like a desk between them. It became an absolute necessity for her to think straight. Never had a man made her incapable of that. She didn't like it, and she certainly didn't need it right now.

She gestured to a chair sitting in front of her desk. He took it, but only after she sat. The southern gentleman aspect of the man warmed her insides and appealed in a way she'd never experienced.

She didn't care if she sounded rude. For her sanity, she needed to keep him at arm's length. "Okay, Detective, you got what you wanted. Say what you need to say."

He cleared his throat and shifted in his seat. It made her wonder if it was her comment, or his assignment on the ship that made him uncomfortable. "I can imagine learning your friend was murdered is hard to wrap your head around, Dr. Brady. For the moment, if you could focus on the work that needs to be done, I'd appreciate it. The captain mentioned I'm going to need a list of the people who worked with Dr. Roberts.

I know you have a lot on your plate, but I do need that as soon as possible."

He was right. A little blunt about it, but right. She needed to access doctor mode and do her job. She stiffened her spine, shoved all her emotions in that special place inside where she kept everything she needed to deal with at a later time, and looked Detective Langdon in the eye. "Of course. I'll do it as soon as I can. Anything else?"

"Yes."

He returned her look for a moment before lowering his gaze and ran a hand around the back of his neck. It had her taking a closer look at him. His color seemed a little unnatural, and sweat beaded his brow. Something wasn't right. Was it connected to the investigation, or was it something completely unrelated? She put the brakes on that train of thought. Professional and distant was how she needed to handle this.

"We're going to be spending some time together as we work on this, and I'm concerned the staff will think it unusual for a senior officer to be seen so often in the company of a low-ranking security guard. I'm not too familiar with how things work on a cruise ship, but I'm guessing it's not the norm."

"You're right." She knitted her brow for a moment. "Since you're the one with experience in undercover, I assume you have something in mind to deal with that."

He nodded once. "I do and your input would be appreciated. Working on board a ship, this whole scenario, is foreign territory for me. On top of which, I don't generally do undercover work so I'm guessing we have something in common there. Both of us are doing a job we don't have a whole lot of experience in. I understand you worked in an ER in Chicago, but you weren't in any sort of management position like you are now."

"That's correct, though as the staff doctor for Caribbean Seas, I was in charge of the crew I worked with for the last year or so. I'm not sure how that matters."

He gave her a crooked smile. "Not a whole lot, really, just trying to get to know you a bit better." His warm gaze skimmed her face for a moment before it hardened, and he cleared his throat. "I'm thinking, in the interests of both of us doing our jobs without drawing undue attention, and giving away the fact I'm investigating a murder, we should pretend we knew each other before we moved to New Orleans. I know the Chicago area rather well as I lived there for a while, and I grew up on Lake Michigan."

She nodded, looking at her fingers as they idly tapped the desk rather than at him. For a moment she yearned with all her heart to have known him in her wild days. In every sense of the word. To counteract the desire, and the squiggly feeling in her stomach the thought engendered, she crossed her arms, and leaned back in her chair. The creaking noise it made in the silence was enough of a distraction to get her thoughts back on track.

"I'm thinking something along the lines of a mutual friend mentioning you were working on a cruise ship," he offered. "I was in need of a change of scenery, so I got in touch with you about a job with Caribbean Seas." He waved a hand in the air. "Be vague about details, I don't think it will matter that much to anyone."

"Hopefully. There's no guarantee my nurse, Celeste, won't want details. We're good friends, as well as roommates when we're not working on a ship."

He pursed his lips. "If you need to add any details to the story, make sure to fill me in, and visa versa. I don't know anyone here, so I doubt it will be an issue for me. Just stick to the facts as much as possible. It makes you believable, as well as keeps things easy to remember."

"Then you might want to know, I don't get involved romantically with the men I work with. That's my reputation, and all that up close and personal you were doing on our way to my office has probably got people wondering."

He raised his brows. "Indeed? Now you've got me intrigued, Doctor."

Good. She clenched her teeth. No. *Not* good. She didn't want to intrigue him. Did she? Still, she couldn't help the small smile. "Perfect. I like to be mysterious."

"Could be dangerous if you want to keep your male co-workers at arm's length. Some of them might be attracted to the challenge."

"A little danger never hurt anyone, did it? As long as you're aware of the risks and prepared for them."

"If I didn't like danger, I wouldn't be a cop. But a doctor who likes a bit of danger... Now that's intriguing indeed."

Her heart began to thunder all over again. Her palms suddenly felt clammy. It took everything she had to keep desire from showing on her face, or in her eyes. To maintain her doctor persona. A little verbal sparring wasn't going to hurt, but if she let on how attracted she was, how often she'd broken the rules back in Chicago, it would be the demise of new Sage Brady.

She uncrossed her arms and sat forward in her chair. "I'll get you the list as soon as I can. Be patient. I have a lot to do before we leave port tomorrow. I'll let people know we were acquaintances in Chicago and I helped you get a job here. Anything else?"

"That's all for now." He stood. "Don't forget to call me Dace, Sage."

Chapter Two

Detective Langdon wasn't the only person in the waiting area. That Sage hadn't noticed had her mood plummeting. The mere sight of him made everything else fade away. Stupid of her to think that might have changed overnight…

So not good when she really needed to focus on her new responsibilities. How would she survive working with him on this investigation? Plus, Celeste wasn't going to buy the 'old acquaintances' routine. At least the part about them being *just* friends. Not when her friend knew Sage had used sex as a way to cope with the demands of being an ER doctor and the stress of trying to impress her father.

Was the stress of her new position, and the death of her friend bringing her old self back to life? Or was it the fact no man had ever attracted and intrigued her the way Dace Langdon did?

She turned to the crew member sitting next to Langdon and forced herself to focus. "Hello, Mr. Devlin. Have you been checked in yet?" She offered her standard professional smile, and an expression tailor-made to put everyone at ease. At thirty-one, with several years' experience as a doctor, it was now automatic.

"Actually, no, Dr. Brady. It's unusually quiet in here at the moment."

"I'm guessing you're here for a drug test."

Her eyes darted to the detective before returning to Sean Devlin, hoping Dace was there in his job as a security guard, making sure Sean followed procedure with the drug test. She hadn't had time to compile the list he asked for, she'd been too busy making sure the infirmary was well-stocked for the cruise, getting the staff work schedule set up, and acquainting herself with her new responsibilities. Which meant she hadn't had a spare moment to mentally prepare herself for any questions he might have about the crew either. She tucked her hair behind her ears and chewed the inside of her lip for a moment.

"Yes. I had to make an unexpected trip home last week, and since I left the ship, the powers that be want a urine drug test before the ship sails. As if random drug tests aren't enough to keep them happy."

She bobbed her head once, though her shoulders didn't relax with the news. "Does that mean you missed out on the staff meeting yesterday?"

"I did. I returned this morning. I feel like I've been running around like a chicken with its head cut off since I got back."

"Then you probably don't know about Dr. Roberts…" Her voice trailed off as she swallowed an unexpected lump in her throat. She hadn't needed to tell anyone what had happened to Eric yet and was surprised how hard it was.

"No. Did he quit?"

She swallowed before shifting into her bearer-of-bad-tidings persona. "Dr. Roberts passed away unexpectedly."

She paused to get a handle on her emotions, but it

was too personal, and try as she might, she couldn't control the tears that filled her eyes. She was still having a hard time wrapping her head around the fact he was really gone, much less murdered. The man who had taken her under his wing, shown her the ropes, and kept her from having a nervous breakdown. She blinked rapidly, rolled her shoulders, and continued in a slightly huskier tone, "So you're looking at the new, though possibly temporary, Chief Medical Officer. Officially, Dr. Middleton is now the staff doctor, and I'll be dealing with the passengers."

Sean paled and swiped a hand down his boyish face, then ran his fingers through his blond hair. The look of sadness in his green eyes mirrored her feelings. Sage was surprised when she first met him to learn he was older than her, not near as young as he looked. "Wow. Rather unexpected. How?"

"Heart failure. You're right, rather unexpected in a fifty-year old, though certainly not unheard of."

The lie tripped over her tongue. No one but her and two others on the ship knew the truth. She'd just as soon be as ignorant as Sean about that, though. *If he truly was ignorant. He'd been absent from the ship at the same time Eric was murdered. Maybe that sadness was an act.*

She struggled to keep her expression neutral. She hated looking at everyone like they were capable of murder. Her colleagues. Her friends. She wasn't suspicious by nature and it didn't sit well. In fact, it made her sick to her stomach every time she thought about someone she worked with being capable of such a heinous act. If she was honest, it scared her a little, too. She admired Detective Langdon's ability to act normal around people when it was part of his job to be suspicious.

The timing of Celeste's arrival couldn't have been better.

"Hello, Celeste. Sean's here for a UDS, can you take care of that for me?"

Both of the men rose.

"Of course, Dr. Brady." She swept out a hand toward the door. "After you, Sean."

"Thanks," Sage said to their retreating backs. Celeste smiled at her over her shoulder.

A movement out of the corner of her eye caught her attention. Lovely. *Now* the receptionist decided to return to her desk. Why couldn't it have been before Sage walked into the waiting room?

She suppressed the urge to fidget under the ice-blue stare boring into her from the other occupant of the waiting area. Pretending they were old acquaintances was harder than expected, and the look he was giving her proved she wasn't doing a good job of it. Failure wasn't an option. Failing Dace and failing Eric if they didn't figure out who killed him. Not going to happen.

She could handle this and Dace Langdon needed to know it. And what kind of insanity was this, wanting him to like her, admire her? Usually sexual tension, and physical attraction were all she cared about. There was no room in her life right now for an emotional entanglement, but, holy hell, there was something in his eyes along with the disappointment, a desire to protect. And she longed to be protected. A need she'd never felt before.

She tucked the back of her white uniform shirt more firmly into her skirt. Bad idea. His penetrating gaze zeroed in on parts of her she'd rather not be drawing attention to and the look in his eyes changed from protective to heated. Pupils dilating, nostrils flaring slightly, as though savoring the scent of her nearness. Her heart rate picked up and a thrill danced the length of her spine. The way he was looking at her now made it a challenge to remain professional, or breathe for that matter. The intense heat made her wonder if it had been so long since she'd physically desired any one, she'd forgotten what it felt like—or if the intensity was unique to Dace.

She squared her shoulders. A test of her ability to resist temptation was bound to happen at some point. She shouldn't be mad at him, either, simply because he happened to be the one to weaken her resolve. He hadn't actually *done* anything other than been given an assignment which forced them to work together. Well, not exactly true. For a moment he'd looked at her like he wanted to eat her up in small luscious bites.

Still, she could *do* this. "Hey Dace, how are you settling into the new job?"

He cleared his throat, blinked, and the look in his eyes was gone. "So far, so good. I appreciate your helping me get the job. I think it's exactly the change I was looking for."

"So, are you here with Sean, or did you need something else?"

"I'm just here to make sure Sean gets his drug test."

She rocked on her heels as she waited to see if he was going to say more. When he didn't, she looked at him in confusion and sucked in a breath through her teeth. She stifled a sigh of relief when Sean rejoined them, and as she turned toward him, he shot her a quick glance before looking at Dace. "Are we good? Passengers will be embarking in a few hours and I need to get to work."

He waved a hand in the air. "Knock yourself out, Sean. Thanks for your cooperation."

She turned back to Dace, intending to make a quick exit, but her shoe caught on the carpet and she stumbled into his arm. The length of it pressed against her from shoulder to thigh and left her feeling felt-up. *How stupid was that?*

His breath hissed between his teeth and he jumped back from her like she burned, backing into the chair he'd been sitting in and barely keeping himself from losing his balance. She grabbed his arm above the elbow to help steady him, but he yanked it out of her grasp, hung suspended for a moment, then collapsed into the chair.

At first, when he seemed anxious to get away from her touch, her self-esteem took a shot in the gut. But then the look on his face set off alarm bells. She sat beside him to lift the lower edge of his sleeve before he had a chance to stop her.

The obviously-self-applied, very large gauze bandage on his bicep was suspicious enough. But his hostility had her hesitating to pull it off and see for herself exactly what was under it. "Well, Mr. Tough Guy, what's going on with your arm?"

He shrugged the opposite shoulder. *Only* the opposite shoulder, she noted. "I was injured on my previous job. If it was something you needed to worry about, don't you think I would have told you already?"

"How about we don't go there? How long ago did

you hurt it, Dace?"

He gave her a mutinous look, which she returned with one of her own. "Think long and hard before you reply," she advised, softly enough the receptionist couldn't hear.

He blew out his breath, and she couldn't decide if it was in frustration or resignation. Maybe it was both. "I don't know. About two weeks."

"If that's the case, I need to look at it. An injury that old shouldn't make a man like you fall on his ass." She raised her voice a little, hoping she came across as annoyed at a friend. "Why didn't you tell me about this when it happened? I'm a doctor for Christ's sake. I could've taken care of it then. What am I going to do with you?"

"I honestly have no clue," he muttered. "What the hell am *I* going to do with *you*?"

Before he had a chance to stop her, she gently but efficiently stripped away the bandage. Her heart sank when she uncovered a ridge of angry red tissue oozing purulent matter. The firmness beneath the skin edges made her bite her tongue in an effort to hold back words better left unsaid. It took several calming breaths for her to stifle her initial reaction to berate him for not seeing a professional sooner.

She schooled her features into a blank mask and took a quick peek at Dace's face. He acted like it didn't hurt, but she recognized the signs of pain in his features. She was trained to look for them. Some guys didn't appreciate the line between tough and stupid. This was worse than she'd suspected. The wound was a deep one, several inches long, running across his bicep. At a guess, the infection had been festering most of the two weeks since it happened. He wasn't going to like her diagnosis.

"What a fine mess we have here, Mr. Langdon. You're going to have to come back to the exam room so I can take care of this properly."

Jaw clenched, he gave a curt nod before he stood. "Lead the way."

****

He knew his injury needed medical attention and he'd planned on talking to Dr. Brady about it as soon as the ship was underway. When it first happened, he thought he could doctor it himself, keeping it disinfected and changing the bandage regularly. It wasn't the first time he'd been cut by a knife and he wielded a gauze roll with the best of them. By the time he realized it was beyond his ability to self-medicate, he hadn't wanted it to jeopardize his new assignment. Time off, no matter the reason, was *not* an option, something he'd made abundantly clear to his boss. There wasn't any information he could attain being on board this ship that they couldn't have found out via email. This undercover assignment was really an undercover vacation. Though to a certain degree he was still part of things and could keep busy working to keep from dwelling on his failure to serve and protect.

Ah hell…

Who was he kidding? He'd known he needed stitches as soon as he was stabbed. He neglected getting the proper care because a nasty scar from a knife wound was much less than he deserved. And a temporarily painful injury that left a physical reminder of the consequences of letting his emotions affect his ability to do his job was good penance.

Now he had to face the consequences. He hoisted himself up onto the exam table, and only then did he notice a nurse had joined them. Where did she come from? He knew better than to get so distracted that he missed important details. Maybe the infected cut *was* starting to affect his abilities. He let his attention wander to the doc, though he knew it was stupid. Seriously, that kind of gorgeous shouldn't be allowed to work on male patients. It was too much to deal with when your health issues wreaked havoc with your thinking faculties. Not that *his* health issues were doing that. But he'd seen the effect she had on Sean and he wasn't even ill. He could only imagine…

Her dark green eyes didn't help things. Each time he was snared by them he felt himself going under; control ebbing away. And that was a very bad thing. He didn't need some froufrou cruise ship doctor making him forget what he was there for.

"I need you to take your shirt off, Mr. Langdon."

Her lips were such a distraction it took him a moment to compute what she said. Which brought home to him that working with her might actually affect his ability to do his job.

"Does your arm hurt enough you need help undressing?

Good God, no.

"Sorry. I can do it. I was just wondering if I should be worried since you have the nurse here. Or is she the one who's going to bandage me up, once you have a look at it?"

He started undoing the buttons of his uniform shirt, then untucked it from his pants and shrugged it off his shoulders. It felt like his arm was on fire, but he ignored it, as well as the silent offer of assistance from the nurse. He didn't want Dr. Brady to know how bad off he was. Which worried him.

Why didn't he want her to see him as fallible? A doctor was one of the few people who needed to know his exact physical condition. This desire to be her hero, to take care of her, make sure she came to no harm, was above and beyond what he usually felt as a police officer. It was too personal and that could be dangerous.

He eyed his shirt and decided his uniform was the number one thing he hated about this assignment. He hadn't been back in the bag in over a decade; it made him feel like a mall cop or some such nonsense. Was cruise ship cop a step above that? It didn't feel like it.

As he tossed the shirt on the table behind him, his gaze collided with hers, and stayed there longer than he liked. Worse than that? His eyes got no further than her mouth where her teeth were biting her bottom lip. A luscious lip he wanted to taste for himself. Teeth he wanted biting *his* lips. Had anyone ever turned him on so quickly? Getting hot and bothered about a woman he had to work with was a recipe for disaster. One of many things he'd learned the hard way as a green police officer. It didn't stop parts of him from being more than ready to—*aching* to in fact—take things to their natural conclusion right there on the exam table. Or maybe that counter on the other side of the room. Of course, that would mean moving all those clear jars full of medical supplies out of the way, which would be problematic…

He mentally swore at himself, then thanked God for small mercies. At least the injury allowed him to keep his pants on.

She donned medical gloves and started probing the

wound with gauze pads and a pair of tweezers. He told himself she was being gentle, but holy hell, it felt like she was digging in his arm with a hot poker. In fact, once he removed sexual attraction from the equation, she did a terrific job of putting him at ease, made him feel like she had everything under control. Although unclear as to exactly why, she *was* making him feel better inside and out. He wasn't even sure how it happened but his admiration for her went up a notch. She was the real deal.

Still...whoa baby, that last jab hurt like a mother.

He ground his teeth together and sucked in a breath through his nose to keep from growling. Thank God she wasn't the one formally in charge of the crew's medical needs. He prayed Dr. Middleton would take over his necessary medical treatment when Dr. Delicious was done with him. He shifted in his seat and the noise of the paper sheet covering the exam table echoed around the room. Or was it an echo in his brain making it seem so loud?

She was talking to him again. *Why was it so hard for him to focus?* Could it be there was something seriously wrong?

"This is Celeste, your nurse, and she's going to get your vitals. Temperature, heart rate, blood pressure. We share an apartment in New Orleans when we're not working on the ship." She cleared her throat. "As I haven't seen her much since you got hired on with Caribbean Seas, I—uh—just told her about you today."

He dragged his attention away from Sage to look at the nurse, wracking his brain to remember if they'd done a background check on her. The throbbing in his arm made it difficult to think clearly, but he was pretty sure they hadn't, though maybe they should have since she worked with, as well as lived with, Dr. Brady. If Sage didn't put her on the list, then he would before he gave it to Rocque. She was a cute little blond, with an open face, but many was the time he'd found looks to be deceiving.

"Nice to meet you, Mr. Langdon. I hope you enjoy working here as much as we have. Now you just try and relax. Sage and I will have you fixed up in no time. And don't let her beautiful exterior deceive you. She's good at what she does."

"I didn't know her real well in Chicago, but I did know her reputation."

Celeste's eyes widened, and the strangled noise Sage made had warning bells going off in his head. Maybe they didn't investigate her history in Chicago thoroughly enough.

"Oh really, Mr. Langdon?" Celeste chirped. "I only have Dr. Brady's version of her life in Chicago. I'd be interested in your point of view."

His brows drew together. He was missing something here, but for the life of him, couldn't get a handle on what. His wound couldn't heal quick enough. He didn't like operating at less than one hundred percent. Still, he had the report on her clear in mind.

"I'm guessing she hasn't told y'all she was reputed to be one of the best ER doctors, if not *the* best, working at her hospital."

"That's enough about me. Dace, the infection in your arm is serious. Based on your flushed cheeks, I'm betting you have a fever." Those green eyes narrowed while Celeste wrapped a blood pressure cuff around his other arm. "Even though Celeste will have that information in a minute, could you tell me if you feel feverish?"

Yes, but not for the reason you think...

He shrugged a shoulder in an attempt to look careless. "I haven't thought about it much, I've been too busy getting myself up to speed for the job. There's a lot more to learn than I thought there would be."

She smiled. "Working on a cruise ship isn't as glamorous as you'd think. You need to be able to work long hours. Full days off are few and far between." She dropped her hands from his arm. *Finally.* "This injury is enough to put you out of commission for quite a while. Has it affected the range of motion in your arm?"

"You want a demonstration?"

"Maybe. I'd like your impression first, though."

He bit back a frustrated noise and ignored his desire to be some kind of macho superhero. It was necessary to give a doctor all the information he could. An injury didn't make him less of a cop. Or less of a man. "I haven't been able to use it like I should for about five days now. I find myself favoring it whenever possible."

She went back to poking and prodding with the tweezers and gauze, with the added attraction of some yellow-brown stuff that smelled like antiseptic. He looked at the jars lined up on the counter and focused on one filled with cotton balls. It reminded him of the big fat flakes of a spring snow. Something he hadn't seen in years. Or missed, until that moment.

"Jesus, Dace." She shook her head at him. "You really should've told me about this right away."

Her voice brought him back to the here and now. Still, he wasn't completely out of it. He could read between the lines on that one. *Why the hell didn't you see a doctor sooner?* He forced his attention back to what she was saying.

"Do you have a high tolerance for pain?"

"Oh, I can tolerate a lot of things, Dr. Delicious, you have no idea."

He gave her the once over, let his gaze linger on her rosy cheeks. He needed to lighten things up a bit. Make sure Celeste bought their old friends routine. Then her teeth sank into her lower lip. He shifted slightly in his seat. Damn, he hated that paper sheet.

She opened her mouth, closed it with a snap and cleared her throat. "Dace, haven't I told you a million times not to call me that? I'll forgive you this once, since we haven't seen each other in years, but if you do it again, I'll hurt you in ways only a doctor knows how. Now, behave yourself. I repeat, this injury is serious."

He gave her what he hoped was a contrite look, but in truth, he wasn't the least bit sorry. Talking with her took his mind off… Everything. As did the flush in her cheeks, and the sparkle in her eyes. "Yes, Dr. Brady. I'm sorry. I'll behave." He winked. "I always follow doctor's orders."

"Now, on a scale of one to ten, where's your pain at?"

He flinched when the nurse stuck the thermometer contraption in his ear. *Damn it.* He'd forgotten about the nurse mere seconds after thinking about her. He didn't answer Dr. Brady's question until Celeste told her the reading on the thermometer and logged it in on his chart. He didn't realize he had a fever. Of course, one degree wasn't worth worrying about. Was it?

Sage pointed at a pain chart on the wall. He

frowned, trying to decide where his pain was at. Over his time as a cop, he'd felt worse. Like after he'd been shot and needed surgery. Yeah, surgery hurt like hell once the pain meds wore off. So, maybe that wound hurt more than this one. Still, he wasn't a wimp. He knew how to push through pain and do what needed to be done. Emotional pain on the other hand... Who knew?

"Five." She looked askance at him and he shrugged carelessly. She wanted a number, he'd given her a number.

"Why didn't you get this stitched up right away?"

He should've anticipated that question and had some pat answer ready. No way would he tell her the real reason. He wanted the pain to remind him not to let emotions get in the way of doing his job, and the scar to make sure he never forgot.

"None of your damn business." He swiped a hand down his face and sighed. *What happened to keeping your emotions out of it, Langdon?* "Sorry. Between the pain, and the stress of learning a new job, I'm not thinking straight. How about we focus on the fact you're taking care of it now?"

"Geez, you two." Celeste shook her head. "How about you save the—*flirting*—for later? After we take care of this injury, which in my opinion, needs to be done ASAP."

He gave Celeste an apologetic look before turning his attention back to Sage. Their eyes met and held, for a lot longer than he wanted them to, and judging by the emotions flitting through hers, she wasn't all that thrilled about it either. His hand clenched into a fist. An unconscious response to an overwhelming need to punch the guy inside him who was unhappy about that. He forced himself to look over at Celeste and nodded his head.

"I appreciate the stupidity involved in not having this treated right away, but I'd like to just deal with the here and now, if we could. What are my options?"

Sage stepped back away from him and gave him a head to toes assessing look. "If you came into my Chicago ER, I'd tell you, you need surgery to fix it properly, as well as a round of IV antibiotics to halt the infection. It could go septic at any moment."

Whoa... No wonder she insisted on taking him to the exam room. "Can we do it right now, or is it something we need to schedule?"

She barked out a laugh, then closed her eyes for a second. "Sorry, that was very unprofessional. Though it's a procedure I could do in my sleep, we don't do surgery on board. You're going to have to take medical leave and go to a real hospital. Fortunately, we haven't left port yet. I'll get the necessary paperwork ready so you still have a job when you're healed up. I'm really sorry, Dace."

Chapter Three

What the hell?
She knew why he was there. Why would she even *suggest* he jump ship because of his arm? Was it personal? Even though she'd said nothing, it'd been clear since the meeting with the captain, that she didn't want anything to do with his investigation.

Was this her way of putting an end to it? Even though he was ninety percent sure his boss had sent him on a fool's errand, *she* wasn't going to put an end to his assignment. Besides, there was that ten percent that he couldn't ignore.

"No."

She looked him straight in the eye, and her concern for his well-being, as well as the seriousness of the situation, came across loud and clear. "What do you mean, 'no'?" She nodded at his arm. "You *want* that to go septic? Do you need to get seriously ill before you do something about it?"

It's not personal. She's just doing her job. His focus darted to the nurse. Damn it. He'd done it again. The nurse. She was a medical professional. Most likely very well aware of the proper treatment for his injury.

If he was honest with himself, he felt like he could go to bed and sleep for a week. But would he? He hadn't had a good night's rest since Donato died. Nothing like a death on your conscience to keep you awake at night.

The discussion he needed to have with Sage couldn't be conducted in front of Celeste, so he lowered his voice. Focusing on her was oddly calming. "How about a consultation? Tell me all my options. In your office, maybe? Alone."

He forced the smile playing at his lips under control as he watched her glance at the nurse and nod her head once. She stripped off her gloves and dumped them in the trash. "That's all for now, Celeste. I'll let you know when I need you again. Why don't you get yourself a snack and put your feet up for a moment?"

Once Celeste left the room, he hopped off the table. The protective paper sheet made a crinkling noise that sounded excessively loud in the silent room. He shrugged back into his shirt but didn't bother buttoning it. Something had to be done about his arm today and the shirt would most likely be coming off again. One thing was for certain, it was *not* going to be surgery in a regular hospital. At least not right away. There had to be something to keep the wound from getting worse until the investigation on board was over, and he could take care of it properly.

When they were seated in her office with the door closed, he stared at her long and hard, momentarily caught off guard by the color that rose in her cheeks when her eyes flicked down to his bare chest and took way too long to return to his face. However, all she did was cross her arms and lean back in her chair. Sexual attraction aside, he sensed the doctor was going to be an asset. If there was one thing he'd learned in the last month it was to never ignore his gut. Because *feelings* had kept him from doing his job the way his gut was telling him to, a young life with so much potential was gone.

My God, how could I let you die, Donato?

It's okay for you to take a break, Dace. To grieve. Donato's death hit you hard. It doesn't make you less of a man. Less of a cop. I don't want to lose one of my best detectives because of it, either.

Could Rocque be right? Or was the fever and infection affecting his ability to think clearly?

He forced himself to concentrate. To try and be the cop he'd been for most of his adult life. His gut told him he could trust her. Which, all things considered, certainly worked in his favor. Besides, he was running out of options. This woman, whether he liked it or not, had the power to get him thrown off the ship. *Not going to happen.*

"Are you going to tell me what this is all about? We can't afford to waste time."

What the...? She knew very well why he needed to be on the ship.

"Even though my assignment on this ship is a joke—."

"A joke*?* What does that even mean? Dr. Roberts wasn't murdered? Does Captain Southerby know this?"

Wow. She was even more attractive when she was angry. How was that possible? He gave a gusty sigh and swiped a hand down his face. "No, no, that's not what I meant. Dr. Roberts *was* murdered. But he was murdered in his home, which means, although it's possible the person who did it worked on board with him, it's highly likely his death isn't connected to his job. I have this assignment because I refused to take time off—."

It appeared one of Dr. Brady's many skills was getting people to open up to her. Or... Was Rocque right? *No.* It was his damn injury messing up his brain. He gave her what he hoped was a sheepish look.

"Long story short, my captain and I had a bit of a disagreement about this murder investigation. As a compromise, we decided it would be best if I was the one to investigate things on board by cruising through the Caribbean as a security guard. I like keeping busy. If you send me to a hospital, I'm going to find myself taking a vacation I have absolutely no desire to be on. I'm thinking as a doctor, you might understand the need to keep busy."

****

Sage sat up straighter, grateful for the formality of a desk between them. He crossed his arms, leaned them on the desk and looked at her earnestly. Was he trying to charm or intimidate her? Did he think she was stupid? She'd confronted men like this and worse, or better, depending on how you looked at it. Hell, she'd taken on her father, the head of the hospital, and won. Not that it felt like any sort of a victory at the time.

She wished he'd button up his shirt. He had the nicest chest she'd seen in a *long* time, and she'd seen more than her fair share. In an attempt to distract herself, she adjusted the photograph of her mother which sat on her desk, putting it an angle where she could see it better. When her eyes went right back where she didn't want them to go, she picked up a pen and jiggled it in fingers that itched to touch things they shouldn't. She longed for an excuse to run her hands over the sculpted muscles of his torso and discover if the hair on it was soft or coarse. Over his wide shoulders, down his biceps—.

Jesus. Was that a scar from a bullet wound by his collar bone? Just the thought of him experiencing that sort of danger on a daily basis upped the ante for her. Old Sage would've propositioned him there and then. And yes, right on her desk. The fact he was her patient notwithstanding.

Take a deep cleansing breath and concentrate. The man has a serious medical problem. She was a medical professional in charge of caring for him. Full stop.

She gave her head a slight shake. He was so right. She did have a driving need to keep busy. He may not have come out and said it in so many words, but the message came through. He needed to be out of New Orleans for a while. She could certainly understand the need to be somewhere else. How would she have felt if, on the verge of getting away from Chicago, she'd been forced to stay, even for just a week? Most likely it would've sent her over the edge, and she'd bet her new job Dace Langdon was a man on the edge. So from where she sat, she couldn't be the one to keep him from what he needed most. She firmly believed a patient should have what was in their best interests physically *and* emotionally. Treating her patients that way, not her father's constant pressure for her to excel, was why she'd been a successful ER doc.

His eyes roamed her face as though looking for weakness. What was it with him? She wasn't the enemy for goodness sake. Though it did make her wonder exactly who was. Himself? His boss? Or some unknown third party? Didn't matter. He was her patient. His health was all she needed to concern herself with. They may be pretending they were friends, but they weren't really, so getting personal wasn't necessary.

"Are you trying to charm me into getting your way? Because you can save us both the time and give it up. Do you have any idea what it's like to work in an ER in Chicago?"

"I can make a pretty good guess. You see a lot of ugly shit and the stress is a killer. I know first-hand what that's like."

A smile tugged at her lips. She set the pen down and relaxed back in her seat. "Why don't you just tell me what's really going on?" She placed a comforting hand on his, ignoring the tingles that buzzed up her arm from the casual contact, gave it a squeeze and slowly removed it. "I can keep a secret and my number one weapon in situations like this? Doctor/Patient Privilege. You have no idea the kinds of things I've had to keep to myself."

She gave him a quick smile then a long, steady look straight in the eyes, and refused to think about how amazing their color really was. Or be enthralled by how they went from icy blue to a warm sky blue when he decided to give in.

He leaned back in his chair and although there was still a cautiousness about him and he kept his arms crossed, his eyes retained their warm glow. "I need you to fix my arm in a way that allows me to stay on the ship." He paused for a moment. "Compared to what my assignments are normally, this job is fluff. If my arm is going to be useless for a while, it's not a big deal. I can do security guard stuff in my sleep and like I said, there's not going to be much to investigating Dr. Roberts' death. In my opinion, I'm here more as a precaution. If the killer is someone he worked with, having a police detective on the ship will prove to be valuable. As well as keep the passengers from having their cruise disturbed by the harsh realities of life."

She nodded. "Glad to hear it isn't anything huge. I wasn't looking forward to the drama. Been there, done that, don't need it anymore. What did you do?"

He stiffened and looked offended. "What's that supposed to mean? I didn't *do* anything."

"I know your type, Mr. Langdon. Over-indulged in your type in my twenties. No way you're doing this fluff job of your own free will. Besides," she gave him a quick smile, "since I'm supposed to know you, any information about you is useful."

He treated her to a half smile. "It's Dace, remember?" He shrugged and the smile left his face and his eyes. "Let's just say I had a choice and it was the lesser of two evils. My boss and I didn't see eye to eye and since he's the one in charge, he gets the final say."

She looked at him for a moment, trying to decide if she should push it, then mentally shrugged. She knew enough now. Any more was tipping it over into personal and she had no need to go there, even if it would help her pretend they were old acquaintances. It complicated things, sucked you in and made you want to go on a joy ride with Detective Hot and Dangerous. Pretending they were friends was more than enough danger for new-and-improved Sage.

"Sure." She tucked her hair behind her ears and got down to business. "As your doctor I need to give you the kind of treatment that's in your best interests both physically and emotionally, and after talking with you, I can see that, though physically surgery is the best way to take care of your injury, emotionally it may not be.

So, to take care of it here, I'll need to do a debridement. I'll give you a local to kill the pain, scrape out the dead tissue and infection, then pack it with iodoform gauze so it can heal from the inside out. It's been too long since you were injured to suture it. You'll need to come in here daily so I can check it, clean it and re-bandage it. You'll also need to do a round of antibiotics."

"Works for me. Do we do it right now?"

She looked at him long and hard, hoping to make him squirm because sometimes she was just ornery that way, but he'd have none of it and returned look for look. To the point she felt a twinge of guilt for giving him a hard time. Because, truth be told, it was her issues that had all these crazy feelings erupting out of the box she'd shoved them into, he was merely an innocent bystander who happened to be the type of male who was her personal form of crack.

"Yes. We need to take care of this as soon as possible, so you're a priority."

He stood quickly, as though eager for her to start digging around in his laceration with a scalpel. "Same room we were in?" She nodded her head. "After you then."

Which was certainly gentlemanly of him, but she struggled to keep it together when she brushed past him as he held the door for her and headed back to the exam room.

Sage hated herself for it, but she was desperate. Not that surgery wasn't the best way to treat his injury, but she'd hoped to get him off the ship. She loathed the idea of looking at everyone and wondering if they were capable of murder, but that wasn't why she didn't want Dace Langdon around. A guy with a rough edge of danger surrounding him was a habit she'd kicked, with no intention of taking up again. It was a test of new-and-improved Sage she feared she wasn't going to pass.

When she entered the exam room, she took a deep cleansing breath, cleared her head, and became the professional she needed to be to get the job done to the best her abilities and circumstances allowed. After calling Celeste to let her know she needed her again, she washed up and prepared her sterile field.

Syringe in hand, she faced Dace, who'd been prepped for the procedure by Celeste. "Trust me when I say this will hurt. I've had rough, tough biker dudes in tears, begging me to stop. Then again, I've had a frail elderly lady barely flinch. I'm going to numb the area with several shots of lidocaine. It shouldn't take long for it to kick in." As she finished her sentence, she started injecting the local anesthetic into the area around his wound.

"*Jesus. H. Christ!* What the hell is that stuff? How can the procedure possibly hurt more than this?"

She paused in her task, one hand on the underside of his bicep, the other holding the needle pointed at the ceiling. "You'd think so. Just tough it out for a few more minutes. It hurts, but it's the lesser of two evils. Trust me. I'm going to be scraping out the infected tissue with a knife and forceps. You *don't* want to feel that."

Again, she injected the edges of the wound in a fast, efficient manner. Again, he swore profusely, so loud it echoed around the room and left her ears ringing. She feared she'd be deaf until tomorrow by the time she had the area numb. She looked over at Celeste, gave her a quick smile. She returned it with an eye roll that had Sage suppressing a giggle.

Surprisingly, and to her relief, she was wrong. He was silent after that, though she was pretty sure his jaw and teeth were going to ache for a while and his palms would carry deep gouges from his fingernails. She stopped herself from asking him to let her doctor his hands as well. Truth be told, she admired his fortitude. Sucking it up when it was clear to her the pain was taking a toll said a lot about the man.

His injury, the infection, had weakened his defenses most likely, so he wasn't operating in top form, and it was rather impressive he had the strength to deal with the added stress of severe pain without another whimper. Not only did her admiration go up another notch, she found herself starting to like the man.

"As a guess, I'd say this is a knife wound, Dace. Am I right?"

Keeping his eyes straight ahead, he gave a slight nod and spoke through clenched teeth, "Got it in one."

"Any idea if the knife was rusty?"

A slight shake of the head came this time. "If you're worried about tetanus, don't be. All my shots are up to date. Stupid not to, in my line of work."

"Good. I don't suppose you'd like to satisfy my curiosity and tell me how you ended up being sliced by a knife?"

He turned his head then, to look at Celeste before he returned his disturbing gaze to her. "I had a run-in with a gang leader. The collateral damage sucked big time, but the asshole is in custody. That's the important thing, right?" He looked at what she was doing to his arm and winced.

"Am I hurting you?"

"No, just a flashback seeing you take a blade to my arm. Will there be a big scar? It looks like you're cutting away quite a bit of flesh there."

Talking about his current injury wasn't a good distraction, but any information she had about it would be useful. She smiled but didn't dare take her eyes off her work to look at him again. Messing up her concentration right now would be a bad thing for Dace.

She compressed her lips. "Since you didn't get it stitched up right away, you'll probably end up with an ugly one. Part of it depends on how well we keep the infection from getting worse and spreading. Still, most likely it'll be worse than the scar from your gunshot wound." Her eyes darted to the scar, then returned to his arm. She *really* wanted to know the story behind that. "Care to tell me how you got it?"

He shifted in his seat and cleared his throat.

"If you're worried about scarring, you might want to keep still. Don't want my scalpel going places it shouldn't."

She paused to give him a quick smile. His eyes lit with the small smile he gave her in return before they darkened and dilated slightly. Her breath caught in her throat at the sudden heat in them, and her belly fluttered in excitement. Holy hell, the man could get her hot and bothered in the middle of a medical procedure. She blinked, took a deep breath through her nose, and returned her attention to his arm. Right now, Dace needed her to do a thorough job cleaning the infection out of his wound. She needed to return to doctor mode.

"I got shot when I was a rookie cop. It was a hard-learned lesson in staying focused on your job. It missed hitting my bullet-proof vest by half an inch."

"Only little bit the other direction and it would've shredded your carotid."

"Indeed. Aren't I a lucky fellow?"

"I don't think sarcasm is the appropriate tone for that statement. You were very fortunate."

"Yes, well, my partner wasn't. She took a bullet in the leg which shattered the bone, and now she's stuck doing a desk job. If I'd been doing my job like I'd been trained to do, it wouldn't have happened."

She looked at him again, the expression on his face pained. This was not a good discussion to be having with him right now. She wanted him to relax and forget about the procedure she was doing. She'd hoped talking about his bullet wound would bring up a story about him saving the day. She paused in her work and laid a hand on his shoulder.

"In the kind of work we do, I think we all make mistakes when we're new, that have ugly consequences. I can't begin to tell you how many things I screwed up as an intern. When you're doing the kind of job that can have long-lasting effects on someone's life, the learning curve sucks big time."

His shoulders relaxed and she was glad to see it. She removed her hand and continued the debridement. "Now, tell me a story where you saved the day."

Celeste chimed in. "Yes. I want a hero story. Then, if Sage refuses to tell you one of hers, I have one for you."

"Now don't you go telling tales on me, girl. I'm the chief medical officer. I can have you reassigned to that ship you hate."

She laughed. "You wouldn't dare. You like

working with me too much. Told me yourself I'm your favorite nurse."

Dace gave a small chuckle. "I can tell you right now, Sage is my favorite doctor. Even if she did just cut off half the skin on my bicep."

"Shut up. I did not! I did, however, remove all traces of infection and now it's time for the iodoform packing. Tell me about how you saved the day once."

"Hell, you're not going to leave me alone until I do, are you?"

"Nope. Most of the cops I know love talking about the heroic things they do. I'm surprised you're so reluctant."

"I'm guessing those cops were trying to impress you so they could get in your pants. I, on the other hand, don't use that tactic to get a woman in bed."

"I'm sure you don't need to resort to such things. I bet all you need to do is crook your finger at them, and they come running." She gave him a teasing smile, and her eyes widened when she looked at his face. Did his cheeks actually turn pink in embarrassment, or was it just his fever? She looked at the back of his neck and it was the same shade. *Well, what do you know?*

"There's no good way to answer that, *chère*, so I'll just tell y'all about something that happened in Chicago one winter before I was a detective. Just so you'll leave me alone, mind you. So, my partner and I were on patrol when the call went out about a toddler who had wandered away from home. We weren't part of the squad sent out to look for him, as it was toward the end of our shift. I still get chills when I think about what could've happened. We were cruising along Lake Michigan, headed back to the station, and I happened to notice something in the water. It caught my eye because it was winter. Not much activity in the water in winter."

Celeste gasped. "Oh my god. The baby was in the water."

"He was. No one had any idea how he got there without getting hit by a car and it's a miracle he didn't drown. Fortunately, he was in the shallows. I don't think he'd been in there long, he was standing up when I spotted him, but a few more minutes and I'm sure he would've gone under and drown. As it was, by the time I got to him, hypothermia was setting in. He collapsed in the water, but I caught him before he went under. His hands and feet were so blue... The kid was only wearing a diaper. I was so worried he would lose his fingers or toes to frostbite. I couldn't resist going to the hospital a few days later to check up on him."

"So that was you, huh?"

"Don't tell me you were the doctor who worked on him. That would be too much."

"No, it wasn't me. I was still in medical school. It was all over the news, though. He was brought to my father's hospital and he told me about him. The boy lost the tip of a finger and a few toes. Considering what could have happened, he was lucky."

"Did the mother get in trouble?" Celeste asked.

Dace shook his head. "No. I met her, she's a good mom. She was beside herself when she discovered he was gone. I guess the little guy was pretty rambunctious. She always made sure the doors were locked and the whole house was baby-proofed. She hadn't left him for long; she was helping his big sister go to the bathroom. She'd done everything she should have. Sometimes things just happen, and fortunately the boy ended up being returned home safely."

"Freaks me out to think what might have happened if you hadn't spotted him. And—Oh my! I just remembered something. Didn't one of the news stations give you a hero award for that?"

"Aw, hell. I should've picked a different story. I forgot we lived in the same area when it happened. Are you about done, Doctor?"

"Yep. Just need to bandage you up."

When she was done, she was rather satisfied with her handiwork considering the patient was a huge distraction. She removed her gloves as Celeste helped him back into his shirt and hoped her worry didn't show on her face as she took in his pallor, the tightness around his eyes and mouth. She wanted to caress it away with her hands. It had been so long since she's felt something more than physical attraction for a man, a concern for his feelings and well-being that went beyond the medical. And the story he just told her didn't help at all.

She was experienced enough to recognize the vibes of sexual attraction, and she wasn't the only one giving them off. It scared her. If he guessed the extent of what he was doing to her, she'd be fighting herself and him. She didn't like the odds on her ability to fight them both. More so under the circumstances. She made sure her features were schooled into her medical-professional mask before she spoke.

"I'm going to prescribe some hydrocodone for the pain you'll have when the local wears off, along with an antibiotic, and I'll need you back here tomorrow so I can check how it's healing, as well as clean and re-bandage it. Celeste will set up an appointment for you before you leave. Since you opted out of the surgery, we need to keep a close eye on it."

"Sorry, Doc, no can do. Narcotic painkillers make me puke and pass out. What are my other choices?"

She raised her brows. "Prescription strength NSAIDS will work, but not as effectively. Or was there something specific you want to take? Ibuprofen? Acetaminophen?"

"Ibuprofen works better for me."

She nodded and turned to the nurse. "Celeste, would you please finish up here, while I fill the scrips for him?"

"Of course."

Celeste smiled and winked at her behind the detective's back. Sage suppressed a groan. She had a feeling Celeste was going to corner her about Dace.

****

"Okay, girlfriend, spill it."

Sage bit back a sigh of frustration and closed her laptop as Celeste sank into the chair on the other side of her desk. Her moment of reckoning had come. Which sucked because she still wasn't sure how she was going to keep her best friend from wrangling the truth out of her. "Spill what?"

Celeste let out a disbelieving snort. "Don't play innocent with me. You know very well I'm talking about your old *friend*, Dace Langdon. From the vibes coming off of you two, I'd say you had a fling with him in your wild days. Did he move down here to see if he could get something going again? And how could you not have recognized him from the news?"

Sage ground her teeth, bit back some choice words and attempted a careless smile as she shook her head.

She almost blew it recognizing his story from the news reports. How was she going to get out of this one? "Believe it or not, I didn't spend much time with him. We knew a lot of the same people, I ran into him from time to time at some of our hangouts, but I didn't see enough of him to connect that he was the hero from the news story. There was too much time between when it happened and when I met him. Besides, I was always with someone else, and he never made a move."

"Which is another point in his favor, but if the things you've told me are true, I'm wondering why *you* never made a move. Considering the sparks coming off you two every time you looked at each other today, I find it very hard to believe you didn't hook up in Chicago."

Her stomach did that weird thing it always did when there was trouble looming. Celeste had spent very little time with them together, all of which was in a professional setting, and she sensed their sexual attraction. It wouldn't be long before other people she worked with started speculating on their relationship. They weren't going to buy the 'old friends' routine for long. The fact everyone knew she didn't get involved with the men she worked with was going to make the time she spent with Dace even more of a topic for speculation.

She let out what she hoped was a convincing laugh and shook her head. "Honestly, Celeste, nothing happened in Chicago, even though I am rather wishing it had. Then he'd be out of my system, which would make my job much easier now. He's very distracting, and he's my patient. It's a line I don't cross now, even if it isn't something I could get in trouble for working for Caribbean Seas."

Celeste looked at her silently for a few heartbeats. "Okay. Fine. I'm finding it rather hard to believe, but I know how much you hate the person you were before you moved to New Orleans. As much as I'd like to see you pursue Dace Langdon, I'll leave it alone. However, feel free to bring the subject up with me yourself!" She gave her a cheeky grin and stood up.

Sage leaned back in her chair and laughed, hoping Celeste didn't detect the relief she felt. "Don't count on it, but if there's anything going on in that department, I'll be sure to let you know."

"Ha! I knew you were considering getting down and dirty with him."

Before Sage could deny it, Celeste was out of the room and closing the door behind her. So Celeste had figured that out too. It was all she'd been considering since she laid eyes on the man. She feared it wouldn't be long before others on her staff started thinking the same thing. Especially since he was going to be in here every day getting his wound checked, and she was never very good at being anything other than her real self.

On the upside, it would distract everyone from figuring out the real reason Detective Langdon was on board.

Chapter Four

Sage dropped onto the couch in the lounge area of her cabin, kicked off her shoes and propped her feet on the coffee table. Her first day at sea as chief medical officer was done. Sort of. The sun had set on it at any rate. She closed her eyes to revel in the silence as she undid several buttons on her blouse, then untucked it from her skirt.

The curt knock on her door made her jump and though she wasn't slow responding to it, a second came before she gained the strength to respond. *God, please don't be anything serious.* She sighed, and muttering to herself, swung the door open to find Dace standing there in worn jeans and a faded black t-shirt, hand raised and ready to knock again.

Not waiting for an invitation, he pushed past her and walked down the hall to the sitting area, turning to face her as she closed the door and leaned against it. It took everything she had to keep her expression neutral so he wouldn't see how thoroughly irritated she was. With herself, because she still tingled from the brief physical contact as he rushed past; with him, for his rudeness, as well as a general irritation at being disturbed. She'd been looking forward to crashing in her cabin long before she was able to leave the infirmary.

"Come in."

He walked over to the porthole and peered out for several long, drawn out seconds before turning back to face her.

Pushing away from the door, she joined him in the lounge, sank back down on the couch and gestured to the chair. "Would you like to sit?"

He shrugged his shoulders before walking over and taking a seat. He looked like hell. "You missed your appointment today," she pointed out. "Is that why you're here?"

He ran a hand through his dark hair, leaned forward and rested his elbows on his knees. "We have a big problem."

Suddenly chilled, she rubbed her arms. "We?"

"The prescription you gave me for pain, did you fill it yourself or did you have someone else do it?"

"I filled it. I thought I told you that."

He bobbed his head. "With what medication?"

She raised her brows but didn't say any of the sarcastic things that popped in her head. Something was very wrong. "A prescription strength NSAID— ibuprofen. You made it clear that's what you wanted."

"You're one hundred percent positive that's what it was? You didn't accidentally grab the wrong bottle, forgetting I didn't want to go with narcotics?"

She did her best to ignore the accusatory tone. "I know for a fact the stock bottle I took them from was labeled *Ibuprofen.* I take prescription drugs very seriously, Detective Langdon." She shifted in her seat. "What are you accusing me of?"

He looked down at the floor, wrapped his hands around the back of his neck and blew out a breath. "Nothing. Not a thing." He sat up and leaned back in the chair. "If I was accusing you of something, I'd be here in my uniform with the Chief Security Officer and hauling you before the Captain." His eyes roamed her face while she fought the desire to squirm. "You might want to take a closer look at the pills in the bottle you poured them from because they sure aren't ibuprofen."

Stunned, she gaped at him. "What are you saying?"

"They're narcotics, Doc. Made me sick as a dog and had me sleeping so long I missed my appointment with you and was late to my shift. In fact, my stomach is still feeling rather dicey."

"It could be seasickness. Have you been on a ship before?"

His jaw clenched and he raised his chin as he tossed the prescription bottle at her. It landed neatly in her lap. So he was a good shot. So what? She picked up the bottle and turned it so she could read the label. It was the one she'd filled and was properly labeled. She opened the lid and looked at the pills.

"You've got to be kidding me." She shook one out into her hand to get a better look then returned it to the bottle, closed it and set it on the coffee table. "That's definitely the narcotic known as hydrocodone. I'm really sorry, Dace. The last thing I wanted was to make you feel worse. Though some manufacturers sell a very different looking pill, the company we buy from makes an ibuprophen pill that looks very similar to hydrocodone. I'd swear on my life I took them out of the ibuprofen bottle." She swiped a hand down her face and shook her head at herself. "I guess Eric's death has me more upset than I thought."

Or she'd been thinking about the detective instead of focusing on her job... Either reason was not good.

55

She should have paid closer attention. She knew better. She'd been trained better.

"I don't know you very well, Sage, but what I do know tells me this isn't a mistake you would make. Is it possible these pills were deliberately put in the ibuprofen bottle?"

She raked the fingers of both hands through her hair. "God, I don't know if I should hope that's the case or not. The pills do look a lot alike, so if you aren't really looking at them, you wouldn't notice the difference. If I filled your prescription out of the bottle labeled ibuprofen and these pills were in there, the only reason I can think of for it would be that someone's smuggling narcotics through the dispensary."

He nodded and stood. "I think a trip to the dispensary is in order."

"As much as I hate to get off this couch, I agree."

****

She had some seriously memorable legs he decided as she went up on her toes to retrieve a bottle out of a cabinet in the dispensary. The movement hitched up her skirt and revealed just enough leg to make him want to push it higher to get a proper look. And feel.

He was *not* going to take a second peek at the tantalizing strip of lower back that was exposed when her shirt rode up with the action. Had she not been sending off such mixed signals, he would've done both, though. *You absolutely would not, Langdon.* She was his doctor. His colleague too. Still, he hoped one of these days he'd get the full view, and seeing Dr. Sage Brady in a swim suit went right to the top of the list of things to experience on a Caribbean cruise.

He shook his head at himself and made a concerted

effort to remain professional. They were colleagues and he didn't screw around with colleagues. Emotionally or physically. It was part of his personal creed, ever since he'd learned the hard way it wasn't worth the trade-off. But, damn, did she have the kind of figure that made a man ache.

Still, there was no harm in looking.

Uncovering drug smuggling wasn't on said list, however. The last several days he'd been feeling pretty lousy and if he was honest with himself, he'd been looking forward to taking it easy, at least mentally. His brain could use a break from the hard stuff. He just didn't need too much time on his hands because then he started to think—about things he didn't want to think about. He'd had it to here with thinking.

The picture of Donato Jackson's lifeless body, covered in blood and crumpled up on the cement floor flashed before his eyes. *Not here. Not now.* Would that image ever leave him alone? He checked out the doctor's legs again and her voice brought him back to the present.

"There's several bottles marked *Ibuprofen.* I'm not sure which one I used to fill your prescription, so I'm going to have to look at all of them."

She pulled out a metal tray, put a glove on one hand and emptied a bottle onto the tray, then pushed the pills around to get a good look at all of them.

Dace knew the smart thing to do was focus on the task at hand, but his gaze wouldn't shift from the curve of her cheek. The slight rosy hue, the way her rich dark hair brushing against her face highlighted her milky skin. Did she burn easily? His fingers itched to smooth the lock of hair behind her ear. Was her skin as silky as it looked? Forgetting the world in something so soft and beautiful felt like the answer to all his problems. His hand curled into a fist to stop himself from doing something he shouldn't.

His eyes worked their way down her neck. Her pulse beat rapidly at the base of it and though he unconsciously noted she was stressed, all he could really think about was how badly he wanted to put his lips on that throbbing vein and savor the taste of her, then kiss his way up and across her cheek to the most tempting mouth he'd seen in a long time.

What threw him for a loop was how hard it was to get past this physical attraction. He wasn't a kid. He had plenty of experience ignoring women who turned him on. There were times his job, or his life, depended on it and he'd perfected the technique of pretending he felt nothing. It must be the infection getting the better of him. He had to literally shake his head to clear it when she finished what she was doing, in order to concentrate on what she was saying.

"This one is all ibuprofen."

She poured the pills back in the bottle, picked up a second and emptied it onto the tray. It was only a matter of seconds before she was spouting some things that were not only unprofessional but very unladylike.

"All these pills are hydrocodone. Which makes me think they're being smuggled under the guise of ibuprofen because the pills look so similar and the regulations on NSAIDS aren't near as tight as they are on opioids. Easy to come by cruising the Caribbean, too, I bet. Especially on this route, as the ship makes several stops in Mexico as well as Belize." She shook her head and the pained look in her eyes made his stomach feel funny. "Someone on the medical staff is smuggling narcotics. Jesus... Do you think it was Dr. Roberts and that's why he was killed?"

"A distinct possibility, Dr. Watson."

She picked up the bottle, a smile tugging at her lips, and tipped it slightly as she dumped the pills from the tray back into the bottle. "Does that make you Sherlock?"

"Stop!"

The smile vanished as she set the bottle down on the counter and looked at him in alarm. "What?"

Two strides brought him next to her and he reached out to pick up the bottle, then thought better of it. "Look at the bottom of the bottle." She picked it up and turned it over. "Do all the bottles have a little black dot on the bottom like this?" He pointed to it.

"No. As a guess, I'd say someone put that there with a permanent marker."

When she lost all color in her face, Dace put an arm around her waist to hold her up. He took a deep breath through his nose, but it didn't have the effect he was going for. *God, her hair smelled good.* Dark and exotic. Like its color.

"You didn't want your fingerprints on that bottle. That's why you had me pick it up, and my fingerprints are all over all of these bottles. How serious is the trouble I'm in?"

He brushed her hair back off her cheek and tucked it behind her ear. It was everything he'd hoped for and more. He didn't want to think about how much his actions were based on personal concern for her rather than an ingrained response to calm someone down.

"Hey now, it's going to be fine. Your fingerprints

are supposed to be on that bottle. You're a doctor with legitimate access to these medications. I just don't want to add my prints to the mix. We need to have a look and see if any other bottles are marked like that."

"For sure. I'll check the rest of the ibuprofen bottles. I guess it would make sense to smuggle more than one bottle of narcotics."

"It could. Depends on why it's being smuggled. Whether it's to make some extra cash, or if they're working for a dealer. Or if it's for personal use even."

When she rested her head on his shoulder, if only for a moment, his stomach did a little flip. Clearing his throat, he dropped his arm and stepped back a pace. She finished putting the pills away, then quickly checked the bottoms on the rest of the ibuprofen bottles. None of which had a mark, and after a quick peek at the contents it appeared there was only the one bottle of hydrocodone masquerading as ibuprofen.

"Anyone besides you and Dr. Middleton have access to the dispensary?"

She closed the cupboard and turned, leaning a hip against the counter as she faced him. A frown marred her forehead as she slowly stripped off the glove and dropped it in the trash. He ignored the desire to smooth it away with his finger. He was treading dangerous ground again. He blew out a breath and raked his fingers through his hair. It sure hadn't taken long for things to get complicated. Two days. *Two fricking days*.

"This can't be happening to me," she muttered as she put the bottles back where they belonged. "I do *not* need this." She cleared her throat, leaned back against the counter, and crossed her arms. "Do you have any idea how horrible this is? Now, not only do I have to be suspicious of my colleagues and turn over a list of them to a police detective, I have to suspect people who are in a position of trust. On top of which, I've had some run-ins with drug dealers in the ER in Chicago. I have no desire to have anything to do with people like that and I'm *working* with one. Scares the hell out of me." She swiped a hand down her face and blew out a breath. "Others besides Dr. Middleton and I have access. Like my best friend, Celeste. You want me to put them at the top of the list I'm supposed to give you?"

He ignored her outburst because it was a normal reaction. Hell, he was glad she didn't have a meltdown. He wasn't sure he could trust himself if he had to touch her again, because what he wanted more than anything right now was to kiss her and make it better.

"At the moment, I think the best course of action is to put the bottle exactly where you found it. Then we'll go to your cabin and figure out what to do. I'll make sure the captain knows about this and see how he wants to handle it after that. Drug dealers are a nasty bunch, as you well know, and whoever is smuggling the drugs may not be working on his own. We need to be very careful here."

She hesitated for a moment and he held his breath.

"All right. Let's go back to my cabin. The thought of the person who's involved in this catching me with my hand in the cookie jar, so to speak, is freaking me out a bit. I want out of here *now*."

Without waiting for an answer, she headed to the door and he barely made it there first to hold it open for her.

Damn it! He wasn't sure if he liked how quickly this assignment went from easy-peasy to intense. The upside? He didn't have time to think about—things he didn't want to think about. And it was a pretty good excuse to spend even more time with Dr. Delicious. A thought that made his heart pound harder for a few beats.

The down side? Once he'd gotten over his initial annoyance, he rather liked the mundane demands of being a security guard. It was a nice change from a job where he was always a hair's breadth away from life or death situations and decisions. But, it meant more time with a woman he enjoyed being around far more than was good for him.

He hadn't wanted an assignment that had him pretending to be something he wasn't. He'd been on the wrong end of deception too many times and it stuck in his craw. Now here he was the deceiver. On top of which, he'd roped the doctor into the deception. Even though Rocque hadn't come out and said it, he could read well enough between the lines. They didn't trust him to handle anything more intense, and he wanted to squirm right now just thinking about how Rocque had said he was too unpredictable. That his team couldn't afford the risk of his falling apart under pressure. God how he hated his colleagues thinking he might let them down when they needed it most and he couldn't convince Rocque, or Sam, his partner, that his dodging the hard stuff on his last assignment wasn't what it seemed.

Could it be he couldn't be trusted to handle things well right now? He'd never doubted himself before. Maybe it was because their lack of faith had him doubting himself. Regardless, he'd needed to keep busy, and now the ship was under way there was no one else to handle this turn of events. So, with the discovery of the narcotics, whether Rocque liked it or not, whether *he* liked it or not, this was no longer a job he could do with one hand tied behind his back.

What made his stomach threaten to turn on him was having Dr. Brady caught in the middle. Because of her job and the information she had access to, her help was invaluable. It was a good decision asking for her help with the investigation, one he would've made himself, but he didn't have to like it any more than she did.

****

She sank down on the couch in her cabin and covered her face with her hands. Someone she worked with, was most likely friends with, was involved in drug smuggling. And possibly murder. If she had that person standing in front of her, she'd strangle them right now. Drugs hurt so many people. And to think someone was abusing the pharmacy she worked in... Again.

Dear God, it could even be Dr. Roberts who'd been smuggling. It would explain why the drugs were still on board. And in a way, a relief. If it was him, she wasn't stuck in the middle of the Caribbean with a drug dealer and a murderer.

She ground her teeth so hard her jaw ached. Wasn't it enough that her father had abused prescription drugs? She made a deliberate effort to relax her jaw. Certainly Eric, who'd been like a mentor, as well as a father to her, hadn't been involved in the same thing? Or worse, making a profit off it?

Her head was seriously muddled. She'd had a lot to deal with the last few days, but before she had a chance to ponder anything, much less gather her thoughts and decide what to do next, Dace started firing questions at her. She pulled her hands off her face slowly. All things considered, looking at him wasn't a good idea.

"When can you get me a list of the people who have access to that bottle? Do you have the other list I need ready? It's unlikely anyone from a crew other than the one Dr. Roberts worked with would leave that bottle in the dispensary, unless they absolutely had to, so we'll keep it at that for now and expand the search if there's no viable suspects in his crew."

"Whoa, slow down there, Sherlock. I've had a lot on my plate here learning the ropes for a new position, and I've been swamped all day. As Chief Medical Officer, everyone on the medical staff reports to me, which means more work. On top of that, I see patients for a couple hours in the mornings and the afternoons. Do you have any idea how many people take a cruise thinking they won't get seasick?" She gave him a quick smile, then sobered. "I'm guessing you don't want said list on paper."

"Nothing on paper. Email it to me, then delete everything off your computer, so if the person doing this happens to go snooping around they won't find anything. The captain gave me your cell number, so I'll text you my address."

He pulled his phone out of his back pocket, typed in the information and sent her the text. Her phone dinged with the arrival of the message as he returned his phone to his pocket.

"Do you keep your laptop here or in your office?"

"In my office usually. I need to feel like I'm getting away from work when I leave the infirmary. I only bring it with me when I'm on call, which I am tonight."

"It might be safer to keep it here when you're off duty. There's no telling who else might have access to your office."

"God, this sucks. The laptop is password locked, but you're probably right. No sense taking chances."

"Exactly. I'm going to recommend to the captain that we wait until we're back in New Orleans to take action on this. Maybe between now and then we'll have solid proof about what's going on."

Dace sank down on the couch next to her and when he put his hand on her shoulder she stiffened. Not because she questioned his motive, but because of what such a small amount of contact did to her heart rate, the sensations that skittered through her from it, even through the fabric of her shirt. She feared what it would tempt her into doing. She hadn't been this low in a long time and the last thing she needed was temptation.

She had no use for the excitement that danced along her spine at the intrigue of the situation either. Then there was the underlying fear that someone capable of murder, or smuggling, or both, was amongst them, possibly watching her every time she went into the dispensary. These people were her colleagues, *friends*, and she didn't want to suspect them of something nefarious. Still, the mystery of it had her itching to sniff out who did it. Much less the fact, whoever was doing this needed to be nailed to the wall. And the way she felt now, she wanted to be the one to do the nailing. She took a deep breath in an effort to dial it down. Her emotions were all over the place with this news and she needed some time to come to grips with it all.

She relaxed into the armrest of the couch, hoping it would dislodge his hand in a way that wouldn't make him think she was trying to get away from him, but when he removed his hand, she ached for a moment to have it back. An ache that had nothing to do with sex and everything to do with the comfort his touch offered.

After what felt like hours, he scooted away to get comfortable at the other end of the couch and narrowed his eyes at her. "You're worrying me a little, Doctor. Are you okay?"

She nodded but the massive lump in her throat prevented her from saying anything. A giant wall of emotion washed over her, stirring up feelings she didn't want to deal with right now, along with the desire to bawl her eyes out over the death of a friend. She hadn't felt like crying since she learned of Eric's death and now her heart hurt like it might explode with the pain of it. Worse than that, all she could think about was her desire to make it all go away by indulging in the delicious hunk of male sitting close enough she could feel his heat. Someone like him could make her feel so good *everything* would disappear and she sensed straight to her core Dace could do it better than any man ever had. Which made the temptation all the more difficult to resist. She clenched her fists, mentally beating down old Sage Brady. She didn't want to be her. Ever again. She was done with the follies of youth and so beyond over letting her father have power over her in one way or another. It hadn't been the solution before and it wasn't the solution now. But, *good god*, it had never been this hard to tell herself no.

The silence dragged on as she tried to pull herself

together, the only noise the faint sound of the sea lapping against the sides of the ship, and the roar of the engines far below them. Slowly she felt herself regaining control, the overwhelming need ebbing away to the point she could cope.

Eventually Dace said, "I saw how hard it was for you to tell Sean about Dr. Roberts. Have you had a chance to grieve for him yet?"

She shook her head, hoping that was why she was so tempted to forget everything with this man right now. She blinked several times as tears filled her eyes. "Not really. It's been too hectic trying to get up to speed taking over for him. He—uh—helped me through some rough times. And I don't mean with learning a new job."

"Aw, hell, don't say anything else. I don't want to know."

She jumped to her feet, turned toward him, and gave him a glare she hoped left a hole in him. Which brought home again how much this guy got to her. She usually didn't react so heatedly when people thought she 'slept her way to the top', or whatever it was he thought had gone on between her and Eric. Why couldn't people assume she worked hard to get where she was? Why did they automatically think she had everything handed to her because she was attractive? Or because of who her father was.

"Don't you dare judge me based on my appearance. And ewww! No. He was like a father to me." And did a better job of it than her biological one. *So not the time to go there. Get. A. Grip.*

"I'm sorry Sage, truly. I know better than that, even though I only met you a couple days ago." He swiped a hand down his face and shook his head ruefully. "Neither one of us are ourselves right now."

She nodded. He was certainly right about that, but she had a overwhelming need to make him understand the role Eric Roberts had played in her life because, crazy as it was, his opinion mattered. Probably more than it should. Still, it could help him with his investigation if he had a better handle of the kind of person she knew the doctor to be. It was an important piece of the puzzle so he could figure out who killed him and whether he was involved in smuggling narcotics.

Chapter Five

"I was on the verge of an emotional breakdown when I started working with Eric. He pulled me back from the edge. Though the actual time we spent together wasn't much, he felt like a father to me. I'm having a hard time wrapping my head around the fact he may have been the one involved in this. Even though it's the best explanation as to why that bottle was in a place where I—or anyone else with the key code—could access it by accident."

He grabbed her fist, gently pried her fingers open, and caressed her palm with his thumb. Instantly she relaxed and didn't resist when he pulled her down to sit next to him, though she stiffened when he let go of her hand to put an arm around her shoulders and pulled her close. His delicious scent surrounded her and some of her tension eased.

"Settle down, I'm not trying to pull anything. Fall apart in my arms now, instead of in the middle of a situation that requires you to be at the top of your game. You don't have the luxury of ignoring how you feel until a better time, escaping into the routine of day to day life. In my experience, you never know when things are going to go south, and buried emotions not only make things more complicated, they can bite you in the ass big time."

Good God, didn't she know it. She'd lived it. Had

he lived it too? Was that why he was on a cruise ship instead of in the middle of the investigation in New Orleans? And he wanted her to settle down? After saying something like that? She was pretty sure she wasn't capable of settling down anywhere near the man, much less when he had his arm around her, pinning her against his hardness and enveloping her in his heat.

"Sage…"

Oh Lord… The way he said her name, like he was savoring it, rolling it around on his tongue, breathing it out like he enjoyed every letter of it. Goosebumps raised on her skin as his breath tickled the top of her head, and she prayed he didn't notice.

She squeezed her eyes shut for a moment and felt the color drain from her face. Eric Roberts was *murdered,* his last moments most likely ones filled with fear. Her head spun for a split second before the shivering started. She felt like she'd been hit by a blast of cold air from opening a freezer door. The muffled hum of the engines and voices from the hall kept her from thinking she was back in Chicago, where the cold seeped into your bones and stayed until spring. Never had she been so grateful for the presence of another human being. She collapsed against him, wrapped an arm around his waist and held on, burrowing into his warmth. She was so, so cold…

The tears started slowly, one crept down her cheek and dripped off her chin. Then another down her other cheek. She wasn't sure when the floodgates opened, but without being consciously aware of it, her cheeks were soaked with them. Inside she was screaming, but all that came out was whimpering and an occasional moan.

It was rather shocking how upset she was. It wasn't as though the man *was* her father, or any kind of relative for that matter. She'd only known him a few years. Was it the shock of knowing someone she cared about had been murdered?

Gradually she calmed, soothed by the steady rhythm of Dace's heart, and eventually other feelings started to surface. The steady beat of his heart. The strength of his arms as he held her. How solid he felt against her. Slowly she moved her hand from where it rested on his waist back toward herself across his abdomen. *God...* The strength covered by that shirt. Her fingers itched to find out what the skin underneath it felt like. She'd had gloves on every time she touched him and she'd only had tempting glimpses of his abdomen. Like it had a mind of its own, her hand went to the hem of his shirt and slid underneath to rest on his stomach. He stiffened. Of course. He hadn't expected her to do that, but his heart started thundering in her ear the moment skin met skin.

"Yes. Oh yes..." she breathed softly. His flesh felt so good. Exactly how she liked it. Solid, warm, soft, with just the right amount of hair to send tingles all the way up her arm.

She lifted her head off his shoulder and looked at him. At those pale, intriguing eyes and saw exactly what she was hoping to see. She ran her hand under his shirt, up over his chest, and rested it on his bare shoulder. Squeezing slightly, using it as leverage, she pushed herself up and did what she wanted to do the moment she saw him. She drank from his lips. Softly at first, then more urgently because one taste and she couldn't get enough. And neither could he, it seemed.

Suddenly he wasn't sitting there passively. His hands took hold of her head, his fingers threaded through her hair, and he deepened the kiss.

She *knew* it. Being with him like this was as earth-shattering as she suspected. She wanted more. Craved more. Was convinced she could never get enough. She threw her leg across his hips and straddled him, pressing herself into his upper body, wanting to feel every inch of him from shoulder to thigh.

His hands moved from her head to her shoulders where they rested for a moment before traveling across and down her back. Her bones turned to liquid and her blood burned through her veins like molten steel. She melted into him when his hands stopped at her hips and pulled her close. Coming up off the couch slightly, he pressed his hips into her.

She dragged her lips from his and buried her face in his neck, needing a moment to breathe, but she couldn't resist the temptation of it, the feel of his scruff against her cheek. She butted her head against it like a cat begging for a caress, and nibbled on his neck. Damn he was the best thing she'd ever tasted. Felt. Smelled.

His groan rumbled through her, every inch of her reverberating with it, making her writhe against him in a desperate attempt to get closer, to be part of him.

"Sage." The breath of his whisper feathered against her ear and she shivered.

His hands caressed their way up her back, stopping at her head to tangle in her hair. He breathed her name again as he pulled her face away from his neck and looked into her eyes. His were the hot, intense blue of a flame and were nearly her undoing as they roamed her face.

"My God…" He moved his hands from her head to her waist, picking her up off his lap and setting her back on the couch next to him. "You have no idea how much I want you right now… Jesus. More than I've ever wanted anyone, I think. The mere thought of stopping this makes me hurt."

He raised a shaky hand and ran it through his hair. It drew her attention to it, and the desire to run her fingers through those waves was so intense she'd done exactly that before she realized it. It was so much softer than she'd imagined, and she had to ball her hand in an effort to keep herself from doing it again.

He sucked in his breath on a hiss.

"We don't have to stop."

Just like that she'd fallen off the wagon. *And she couldn't care less.*

"Hell, woman, I'm hanging on by a thread here. We cannot do this right now. You're overwhelmed with all sorts of emotions that have nothing to do with me. Trust me, deciding to jump into bed right now would not be a good idea. Not that I'm saying it isn't going to happen. One taste of *you* is definitely not enough. Just not now. Not while we're working together. I don't need that kind of baggage and I'm pretty sure you don't either. We can pursue this—thing—between us later, when I have a new assignment. When we're not working together anymore."

For a few moments all she could hear was the ticking of the clock that hung on the wall over the sofa. The sound magnified in her head and became synchronized with her heartbeat. She buried her face in her hands. Hands that were shaking, she wanted him so badly. But he was so right. She took a deep breath and tried to hold back tears. He'd just saved her from herself, and he had no idea how huge that was. It was pretty weird too. No man had told her 'no' when she made it clear she wanted him. And instead of feeling awful about herself and rejected, she felt grateful. *Grateful.* He hadn't put an end to it because he wasn't interested in sex, or because he wasn't interested in sex with her, but because it was the smart thing, the best thing for *them*. Right now. In this moment. As for pursuing it in the future. She couldn't even begin to think that far ahead in her life right now. She had too much going on in her present.

She took a deep shuddering breath, stood up and walked over to the porthole, letting the rhythmic waves of the Caribbean sooth her. Which it did, but it didn't stop the tears. Wiping them from her cheeks, she turned back to face Dace.

She heard him catch his breath when he saw she was crying again. "Sage… I'm not rejecting *you.* Do you have any idea how hard it is for me to sit here right now and not pick you up, take you into the bedroom, and stay there until tomorrow, or next week even?"

"Thank you." He gave her a confused look. "Thank you for saving me from myself. For doing the right thing. For not taking what was on offer because it was *me* offering it. You have no idea how wonderful it is to have a man turn me down because he knows it's the best thing for *me*, even though it makes him miserable."

Dace stood, straightened his shirt—though not before she had a brief, tempting view of his impressive abs—and shoved his hands in his pockets. He stayed in front of the sofa. "Woman, I have no idea what you're talking about. Are you going to be all right?"

"I think so. For now." She bit her lower lip. Why did it matter so much that he understood why she'd come on to him like that? She twisted her hands together, then ran her fingers through her hair.

He gave her a confused look. "Do you want to sit back down?"

"God no. Having that coffee table between us is a good thing right now."

She shoved her hands in her pockets and started slowly pacing back and forth. She glanced at him as he sat back down. "There's something you need to know, since we're pretending we knew each other in Chicago." She took a deep breath. "Being an ER doctor in a big city is pretty intense. When I first started, I thrived on the action, facing life or death situations, and being able to save someone against nearly impossible odds. It made me feel alive, made me feel special, at times even god-like. It's the sort of job that makes you want to play hard too. See how much you can get away with. Sometimes you just need to let off steam. Then there's the times when you fail to help someone and everything goes south. That creates a need to let off steam too. I used sex to cope."

She cleared her throat and suppressed the memories of the stupid things she'd done, things that had put her job at risk. She was actually being rather stupid right now, but she couldn't help it. She felt compelled to tell him why she'd just thrown herself at him. That it was more than a moment of grief. Was she warning him about the possibility of it happening again, hoping he'd take the high road a second time and not take advantage of her weakness? So she wouldn't have to fight them both? Because being in close proximity with him on a daily basis was beginning to look like something she couldn't do without it resorting to a physical relationship. She swallowed. Did he really have that kind of power after such a short time? She stopped pacing and looked at him. Drank in the picture he made. Hair mussed from her fingers, the expression of compassion on his face, softening the dark and dangerous look he usually wore. His good arm was propped on the back of the sofa, while he rested his other hand on his jean-clad thigh.

He narrowed his eyes. "I don't think we should be having this discussion, Sage. I understand the things people do to cope with what we see and deal with in our jobs. We've all handled it poorly at one time or another. You're upset right now and I don't want you to say something you'll regret later. We have to work together. And when I say that, it includes our pretending to know each other before. It's part of the job and you need to look at it that way too."

She collapsed into the chair. Did he really get it? Regardless, she couldn't help but admire a man of such caliber. The level of concern he'd shown for her when they hardly knew each other. The fact he wasn't going to judge her for what she just revealed about herself. The fact he was trying to keep her from saying something she shouldn't. Before she could respond he continued.

"In a lot of ways our jobs are similar. I know that need to let off steam. To forget. Even if it's just for a few hours. And someone who looks like you? Doing what you do? All you have to do is look at a man and he'd come running."

"Well, yeah, pretty much."

She knew her weaknesses. Didn't ever want to give in to them again. She was tired and overwhelmed by everything he'd told her right now. He was right, he didn't need to know her story. Celeste was the only one who knew that. Still, he'd guessed some of it, so she felt the need to say something. To make it look better than it was. She pressed a hand into her stomach, trying to settle it. The last couple days were starting to catch up with her.

"At first I tried doing the whole relationship thing, but it was so much work. I was so emotionally drained from my job that I gave up trying to build a relationship and drifted into just trying to feel good and forget." She bit the inside of her cheek. "I don't do that anymore. Never again."

He didn't need all the gory details, he'd just told her he didn't want them, and she certainly didn't want him know it had reached the point where she stopped caring about the *man,* and whenever the guy she was with suspected he was being used—or that one time she'd been cheated on—she moved on. Until that morning she woke up completely burnt out, in bed with a man who was really good at giving her a wild ride in the sack, but she knew absolutely nothing else about. She hadn't cared about him as a person. His needs, his wants, his dreams. *So* not her—or the her she wanted to be. She was *not* going to be her father's daughter in that respect.

She was a doctor, like her father, but had become one because she cared about people, wanted to help them whatever way she could. Use her skills and knowledge to figure out what was wrong and make it right. But it was that very same drive that turned her job into a major stressor, and the only way she'd known to cope was by doing something that made her feel good for a few hours. Many people turned to drugs for that kind of escape. Not her. She wasn't her father's daughter in that respect. *No way*.

She'd used sex, with whomever she was attempting a relationship with at the time. When the reality of what she was doing hit her, she walked away, from her job, her city, her life, and promised herself she'd never use sex as a way escape reality again. Because abusing something as a means of escape did make her like her father. Not. Happening. *Ever*.

She pressed her fingers into her temples, closed her eyes, and blew out a breath, suddenly feeling all kinds of stupid. Dropping her hands, she opened her eyes to see him nod once. They looked at each other in silence and she searched his face for any kind of sign he'd judged her and found her wanting. All she found was sympathy and confusion, and the relief was overwhelming.

"So-ooo, is this a roundabout way of telling me you have no intention of sleeping with me? Since that kiss said something completely different?" She shook her head and looked at him again. Only then did she notice the teasing light in his eyes. "Ha ha."

"Aw, hell Sage, I'm sorry." He swiped a hand down his face and released his breath in a whoosh. "I appreciate your telling me this. Really. Since Celeste knows your past it's probably a good thing if I do too. Suffice to say I'm not operating on all cylinders right now either. Truth is, we've got bigger problems to deal with at the moment. Let's just focus on that and forget the rest of this until I can figure out if Dr. Roberts was smuggling narcotics, or if someone else on the crew is involved."

She knew what he was saying should make her feel better, but it didn't. Regardless, she couldn't deal with it at the moment, so he was right about that. She'd deal with it later. "Do you think another doctor was in on it with him?"

"Hmmm... My guess is, no. It's more likely if Roberts was smuggling, it was because he wanted to earn a little extra money selling prescription drugs to a dealer in New Orleans."

"It's not as easy to take drugs on and off a cruise ship as it used to be, but it wouldn't be as hard for a doctor to get away with it since we move a lot of them through the clinic, restocking supplies and such." She shook her head. "It's just so hard to believe he would do it."

"Maybe he had a lot of debt, or was hoping to take an early retirement, or a dozen other scenarios. Trust me, you never really know with people. With the right motivation, good citizens can do some crazy things."

He paused and slowly ran a hand across his chin, the rasp of his stubble sending the same zing through her nerve endings that rubbing her face against it had.

"What concerns me more right now is, if someone else is doing this other than Dr. Roberts, or if he was working with someone on board, they may be in panic mode wondering what's going to happen if the drugs are found and can be linked to them. If Roberts had a partner in New Orleans, they'd be wanting to tie up loose ends, and may even be on board right now as a passenger to do that. In my opinion, if he was smuggling narcotics it's a good possibility he had a partner who murdered him. I can't begin to tell you how many times I've seen greed or disagreements on how to do something, end in one partner murdering another. And, if his partner was another crew member, they could be watching you, wondering if you've discovered the drugs or any other kind of evidence because you have access not only to the pharmacy, but to Roberts' office, and could come across anything he might have in there that would connect them to the crimes."

He paused and put a finger on his lips for a moment. "Actually, if Dr. Roberts was working with an employee who doesn't have access to the drug dispensary, it would explain why that bottle is there for anyone to run across. They'd have no access to it without him."

"Seriously? And that's not going to put my stress level through the roof?"

"I know, Sage. I *know*. So let's focus on what we can do. For starters, like I already said, I need a list of all the people who have access to the dispensary. Then I'll have an idea who else could be involved in this and can keep an eye on them. It could even be the flip side of everything, and the person doing this thinks hiding them in plain sight in the dispensary is the best way to cover up what's going on. And they're willing to take a chance that, if the hydrocodone does get dispensed, no one will notice they're narcotics and not ibuprofen. If they're willing to sell narcotics to the highest bidder, they probably don't care if someone gets them by accident. It's easy enough to replace them at the next stop in Mexico, or wherever."

She nodded and tucked her hair behind her ears as

she thought about her medical team. "We work a rotation of four months on the ship, then we have six weeks off. The staff here right now aren't the ones who worked two weeks ago. We live on board one ship for four months at a time, but we can be assigned to any ship in the company after we come off our six week break."

"Right. So it sounds like what I need, to start with, is a list of the people who were on the latest rotation with Dr. Roberts. Is the rotation a little mixed up because he passed away? Have you been on the same rotation as the rest of the crew?"

She held up a hand in a 'stop' gesture. "Slow down with the questions there. The medical staff is usually all on the same rotation. I'm not because of Eric's death. I wasn't originally assigned to be part of his crew. So everyone has done a couple of cruises already. Which means Eric made a brief visit to his house while the ship was docked between cruises. That in itself is odd, because generally we don't go home while we're in port. There isn't time." She paused, swiped a hand down her face, and squeezed her eyes shut for a moment. "My first year with Caribbean Seas I worked with Eric. He was the Chief Medical Officer." She shook her head slightly in unconscious denial. *Eric smuggling drugs?* It was hard enough dealing with the fact he was dead. "As for the names… It's at the top of my list of things to do."

Before she had a chance to continue, her phone went off. Annoyed with the interruption, she picked it up off the table and went into her bedroom for privacy. By the time she returned to the lounge, drug smuggling had taken a back seat. "There's been a dancing accident in the Floating Lounge on the upper deck."

"Well, now I'm curious. What exactly do you mean by 'dancing accident'?"

"A passenger hurt himself trying a dance move he probably shouldn't have. Do you mind coming with me in case I need help moving him? The nurse feels it's serious enough he shouldn't be moved until he's checked by a doctor, but if there isn't a problem, I may need your help getting him off the dance floor so the guests can continue enjoying themselves."

"Happy to help. And it's probably good for our cover to show up together."

Chapter Six

Dace Langdon didn't come across as someone who cared a lot about strangers, but in the space of a few hours he proved her wrong twice. A few minutes after they arrived in the lounge, the nurse received a call for an emergency several decks below. Since Dace was with her, and emergency medical training was part of the job requirement for a security guard as well as police detective, Sage told the nurse to answer the call and leave things in the lounge to them.

The patient, Zack Freidman, whose anxious wife knelt next to him, slipped while trying out a new dance move, and hit his head on the floor.

One look at the situation and Dace retrieved a blanket to cover him up. Where he conjured it from, she had no clue, but Sage was pretty sure the thankful look she gave him showed her surprise as well, because he scowled at her. "What?"

Shaking her head, she turned her attention back to the patient, annoyed Dace had distracted her from her job so quickly. "Hello Mr. Freidman, I'm Dr. Brady and this is Mr. Langdon, an off-duty security guard I roped into helping us. He's my muscle if I decide we can move you off the dance floor without a stretcher. Can you tell me if anything hurts?"

"My head and I think I twisted my right arm trying to catch myself. I feel like I'm going to black out when

I try to get up."

In case he had a spinal injury, she wasn't going to move him until she knew more, and Dace did what he could to expedite things. He made sure the crowd which had gathered around them, moved far enough away so there was plenty of room for them to work. He also had her emergency medical bag ready for her. She took what she needed from it to take Mr. Friedman's vitals and compared them to the nurse's results, then checked his pupils to make sure they were reacting properly. Who knew Mr. Tough-Guy-Detective would make such a good nurse? She mentally shook her head at herself, annoyed that Dace was a distraction whether he was her patient or her nurse.

"Do you remember hitting your head?"

"Yes. It hurt like hell when I hit the floor, but now my arm hurts so bad…" His voice petered off.

After examining his head and arm, she took his vitals again and Dace handed her what she needed before she had to ask. Calm, efficient, and keeping the patient that way while she worked. She couldn't decide if she liked the connection they had or not, because she didn't need something else drawing her to him. Personal issues aside, though, having him there was the best decision she'd made all day. She bit back a sigh of relief when she finished her assessment "Mr. Langdon, it's safe to move Mr. Freidman off the dance floor. Let's get him out of the way so the passengers can continue to enjoy their evening."

She gave Dace an apologetic smile, figuring he hadn't expected to be doing something like that at the end of his workday. Her heart skipped a beat when rather than looking annoyed, he smiled and winked at her before he moved closer to the man so he could help him up and off the floor. She assisted him, trying to do the bulk of the work because the last thing she wanted was to be the cause of Dace doing his own injury more harm.

He disappeared as soon as the medical assistance she'd called for arrived to transport Mr. Freidman to the clinic where she could give him a more thorough examination as well as bandage his arm. She should be glad Dace had left her to it. She did *not* need to be feeling so bereft after he was gone. He was starting to take over her thoughts far too much lately. She shouldn't be dwelling on the way his arm felt around her shoulders. Or the way his lips tasted. Or the way her skin tingled when he looked at her. Or how in sync they'd been helping Mr. Freidman.

It was over an hour before she was able to return to her cabin, the patient's arm bandaged, and a list of care instructions given to his wife so he could spend the night in the comfort of his cabin rather than in the ship's infirmary. So for the second time that evening she threw herself down on the couch, only this time she was in some comfortable clothes, thank goodness. Now she was so tired she didn't have the energy to get something to eat.

She was glad she had a good reason to miss the formal dinner with the passengers. Not that she minded getting to know some of them in a relaxed environment. Normally she enjoyed it, and a friendly staff was the order of the day on a cruise. She just wasn't up for socializing after the bomb Dace had dropped. She needed time to regroup, and now that she wasn't distracted by medical things, her thoughts went right back to drug smuggling and Eric.

She couldn't reconcile the Eric she knew with one who'd be involved in illegal activities, never mind the fact he could've been in deep enough to get killed. Generally, she was very good at reading people. It helped tremendously as an ER doctor when time was of the essence. Maybe she was worse off than she realized when she quit and had latched onto the doctor like a drowning man grabs a life preserver. He'd definitely been her savior.

She groaned when a knock sounded on her door, for two reasons. It meant she had to get off the couch, and worse, it was most likely Dace. God how she wanted that man. And in the last hour away from him, even though she'd been dealing with a medical emergency, her desire hadn't cooled one bit.

****

He was greeted with a scowl when she opened the door to him, but it soon disappeared when she saw the tray in his hands. He had no use for the thrill that zipped through him when the scowl disappeared. Especially since he knew it wasn't him she was happy to see, it was the food.

Without a word she opened the door all the way, beckoned him in, then turned around and headed back into the living area of her cabin without making sure he followed. Which was okay with him. She'd changed out of her uniform and was wearing some sweat pants cut off at the knees which clung enticingly to her hips, and a tight fitting t-shirt which left little doubt she wore nothing underneath it.

He went from enjoying the view to stifling a desire to drop the tray, grab her from behind and haul her into the bedroom. The speed with which she turned him on was irritating, since making love to her wasn't an option, and he scowled at himself.

She indicated he should put the tray on the coffee table. "Hey, you don't need to glower at me like that. I didn't ask you to come by."

"I know. Sorry. It's not you, so ignore my mood." Well, it was her, but not in the way she was most likely thinking. "I brought you something to eat since you missed dinner. You seemed pretty wiped out, and I didn't think you'd want to go anywhere else tonight."

She made a sweeping gesture down the front of her with her hand "You got that right. As you can probably tell by my outfit."

It took everything he had to keep his eyes on her face. Knowing beyond a shadow of a doubt she wasn't wearing a bra was *not* a good thing.

"I can't help but wonder, though, if there's an ulterior motive to your coming by?" She sat down and pulled the tray of food in front of her, then waved her arm to indicate he should sit too. "We're not allowed to take food to our rooms, you know."

"I know. I have connections."

She wrinkled her nose. "Whatever. I have connections too. And perks for being a senior officer, so we're off the hook either way."

He ignored his desire to plant himself next to her, close enough they could touch, and took the chair instead.

"And yes, I have an ulterior motive. More than one actually, but that one's off limits so let's focus on the other." His voice petered away as he watched her lick her lips to snag some food that hadn't made it all the way into her mouth. It turned him into one giant throbbing ache. He jumped up and went to look out the porthole in an effort to distract himself and collect his thoughts. Not that he could see much other than his reflection since it was dark outside.

"Dace, you're freaking me out a little. Why are you here?"

He clasped his hands behind his back, but didn't turn around. He wasn't quite ready. Or he was more than ready, depending on how you looked at it. "I've got a plan of action, the first thing being, as soon as you've eaten we need to go back to the dispensary and count how many pills are in that bottle. I'd like you to keep tabs on it, see if the bottle stays in the same place, monitor it so we know, if Dr. Roberts didn't put it there, whether or not the person who did is using the pills for themselves, or smuggling them to make a quick buck. It could also tell us if anyone else uses it to fill a prescription. Which is probably information you would need in an emergency."

"I am a little nervous about having the bottle in there where someone could accidentally end up with hydrocodone and have a bad reaction. I'm trying to figure out a way to keep that from happening without making whomever put it there suspicious. That is, if it wasn't Dr. Roberts who did it. The best I can come up with is making sure it isn't easily accessible and checking regularly to see if it stays where it's supposed to."

"That may be all you can do for the time being. It's only a five day cruise and there's just a few days left until we're back in New Orleans where it can be taken care of without causing problems for the passengers. It can give us a chance to figure out who put it there too. For now, without more information about what's going on, keeping a tight watch on it should be enough." He unclasped his hands and turned around. Digging in the pocket of his jeans, he pulled out his prescription bottle. "Here's the pills you gave me."

"Wait a minute. Last I saw they were on my coffee table."

"Yeah, well I didn't think it was a good idea to leave them there so I put them back in my pocket. Now I want you to put them back in the bottle you took them from. I only had one of them. Would you be able to replace that one so the count in the ibuprofen bottle is the same as before you took them out?"

She pulled the fork slowly out of her mouth, set it down, grabbed a napkin and looked at him as she wiped her mouth. "That will be tricky. Though it's not as strict here as it was when I worked in the ER, the drugs are logged and monitored to prevent theft. I don't need that kind of trouble. If I take a hydrocodone out of the proper bottle, my numbers will be off. Which may or may not go noticed. Either way, it would make me pretty edgy."

He nodded, set the bottle on the table, and sat back down in his chair.

She slapped a hand to her forehead. "My god, Dace, you sure mess with my head." She bit her lip and looked away for a moment. "I'm sorry I didn't think of this before. Are you going to need some actual ibuprofen? How are you doing with the pain?

"Some scrip ibuprofen would be greatly appreciated. The over-the-counter ones I brought with me are about gone since I've been taking a higher dosage. If it helps with the count, you can replace the pills you gave me with what I was supposed to have minus one, then take that one and put it in the imposter bottle. Hopefully the culprit won't realize it isn't hydrocodone if he decides to count his pills. I'll be short a pill, but it shouldn't be a big deal since you can write me another scrip if I need it, can't you?"

"Sure."

"Is it going to look suspicious if you go to the hospital again tonight?"

She shrugged a shoulder. "I'll think of an excuse if I need to, but I'm on call until midnight, so it shouldn't be a problem. Were you thinking of coming with me?"

"Yes. I don't want you by yourself. If someone on board was working with Dr. Roberts, or if the smuggler wasn't working with him, and they killed him because he discovered what they were doing, they might get suspicious about what you're doing there, and turn on you."

She rolled her eyes. "You worry too much. I don't need a babysitter. I'm the Chief Medical Officer, my being there isn't a big deal. Even when I'm not in my uniform. Which I will not be putting on until tomorrow unless I absolutely have to."

"I'm coming with you. End of story. I'm not having your death on my conscience as well. I can be your excuse for being there if you like. If we run into anyone, you can say you have to change the dressing on my arm because it's bled through."

"All right."

He narrowed his eyes, a little suspicious about how easily she gave in. She set down her silverware on the now empty plate and stood up. As she walked around the end of the table, he stood up as well. Catching him by surprise, she lifted the sleeve of his shirt to expose the bandage. "Which is apparently true. Between lifting me earlier and helping Mr. Freidman, the wound's started bleeding again. I should've known better than to let you use it like that." She exhaled wearily. "Let's go take care of business."

She headed to the door and he couldn't help but admire her figure as he followed her out. He made sure it was locked because as far as he was concerned, it didn't hurt to be too careful. There were worse things.

It didn't take long to do what they needed to at the clinic, and the first thing he did when she gave him his prescription was take one. He'd hoped the faint nausea since he woke up from his bout with the hydrocodone was left over from his reaction to it, but by the time they returned to her cabin he wasn't able to deny it any longer. He was seasick. And taking that pill on an empty stomach was a huge mistake. How many other ways was he going to come up with to humiliate himself in front of this woman?

His initial plan was to leave her at her door, make sure she was locked in and return to his cabin to wallow in his misery. Nothing in his life had been going according to plan lately, and spending two days with his head in a toilet had not been anything near what he'd planned on with this job. "I need to use your bathroom. Do you mind?"

She looked at him suspiciously, which he didn't blame her for. Asking to use her bathroom when his wasn't all that far away, did sound like a lame excuse to get into her room. Worse than that though, was the narrowing of her eyes when she figured out what his problem was. She stepped out of his way to let him enter first.

"Hope you make it."

He did. Barely. Then ended up staying there longer than he liked. If she'd asked him, he would've told her to leave him alone, but she didn't ask. She was just there handing him a wash cloth to wipe his mouth, placing a cool cloth on his forehead when he took a moment to breathe, asking if he was done or if he was going to go another round. He *liked* having her hand holding the cloth to his head and the other one soothing his back. Who knew?

And when it did finally come to an end, she had a cold glass of water for him to rinse his mouth. After taking care of business, he joined her in the living room where he found her sitting in the armchair. Grateful for that, he stretched out face-down on the couch. Which wasn't really long enough for him, but was better than sitting. He just wanted to be prone for a while. He closed his eyes which seemed to help.

"It can take a while to get used to being at sea. Would you like me to get you something for it?"

He groaned. "No. It was the painkiller on an empty stomach that sent me over the edge. Let's see if it goes away in a bit."

"Your call." There was a long silence before she continued. "You can lie in my bed for a bit if you'd like. You can't be comfortable where you are."

He stifled another groan at the thought of moving. The rolling of the ship was more than enough at the moment. "I'm good. As soon as my stomach's settled, I have a plan for tomorrow we need to discuss, then I'll head back to my cabin."

He wasn't sure how long he laid there. He tried to distract himself from the motion of the boat and the throbbing in his arm by thinking of other things. Dwelling on that explosive kiss with the doctor helped but thinking about her had other parts of him aching, which didn't really help his overall situation. Not with her sitting a few feet away and more than willing to alleviate that particular ache. An epically bad way to cope for both of them. He didn't want to think about the mess which landed him in this job; he'd gone over that particular scenario in his head too many times. He could beat himself up all day long for his obsession with taking down that loser, and how said obsession resulted in innocent people getting hurt and killed. All it got him so far was this lousy job. Now he was face to face with a situation which put another innocent person at risk. Nope. Not thinking about that either because it had him wanting to puke again. Best just turn off the brain, and zone out for a bit.

****

She tried several times not to look at the yummy piece of masculinity sprawled across her couch, but after several attempts to distract herself, including cleaning the bathroom, she gave up. The poor man was in bad shape, the fact he'd zoned out on her couch for over an hour proved that. His arm had to hurt like nobody's business, and he had yet to be able to take something strong enough to get a handle on the pain. Which proved he had a high threshold and was probably what made him so good at his job. She bet he was rather perturbed at looking vulnerable in her presence. Which left her admiring how he dealt with that as well. He didn't turn all macho on her or try to prove himself superior in order to compensate. Not a chauvinistic bone in his body. Which she liked. Probably too much.

She had no problem with letting him rest on her couch; at this point she wanted nothing more than to collapse on her bed. It was past midnight, she was no longer on call, and she'd reached her limit. So, although his spending the night with her would likely complicate things, she stood, intending to head for her room.

The movement was all it took. His eyes flew open. "How long have I been lying here?"

"Over an hour. Feeling any better?"

He rolled over slowly and sat up. "Enough to make it to my cabin. I'm on duty early tomorrow and need some sleep. As do you, I'm sure."

She sat back down. "You said something about a plan?"

"Ah, yes."

He swiped a hand down his face then pushed his hair off his forehead. She looked longingly at that hair, wishing it was her fingers running through it, and almost didn't catch what he said when he continued speaking. "We dock in Cozumel in the morning."

"Yes. I probably won't be seeing as many patients tomorrow so I'll have a chance to come up with the list of people who have access to the dispensary."

He nodded. "Because of the drugs we found, the captain is doing what he can to learn the alibis of everyone on the medical staff without appearing to be fishing. I'll get that info from him tomorrow. After I cross-check it with your list, hopefully I'll come up with a list of viable suspects for my boss. I'd like you to keep an eye on everyone you work with in the clinic while you're on duty. See if anyone acts differently or out of character, anything suspicious. Even if it seems odd for no apparent reason. I need to know who it is, and what it is."

She blew out a frustrated breath. "I hate the idea of looking at all my colleagues like that. I'd much rather not know."

He gave her a sympathetic look. "I know. I'm really sorry you got caught in the middle of this." He ran a hand through his hair again and muttered, "You have no idea how much." He shook his head. "However, it is what it is. My job tomorrow is to keep an eye on the passengers getting on and off the ship. I specifically requested this assignment so I can get a good look at everyone. Any crew members who seem suspicious, for any reason, I'll probably send in for a drug test. I'll also be taking a close look at the passengers. Mexico is the perfect place to pick up cheap narcotics without a prescription, in addition to illegal drugs. Odds are someone's going to try and get away with smuggling. Either for themselves or to make a quick buck. Were you planning on going ashore?"

"Not this stop, but I've been thinking about spending my afternoon off ashore when we're in Belize. It helps to get away from everything for a few hours, even if I don't have the amount of time I'd like to spend there."

"I've got time off then, too. We should spend it together. Being away from the ship is a good time to compare notes without worrying about being overheard. Plus, it will help solidify our relationship in the crew's minds." He stood and looked at her inquiringly before making his way around the coffee table to stop by her chair. As he towered over her, she felt at a disadvantage. She stood as well, though she had no use for the thrill of his proximity, it was an improvement over sitting.

"Are you asking me?"

"I'm not your boss. You decide what you want to do. However, the captain did say you were supposed to cooperate with me."

She rolled her eyes. "Okay, that leaves me no choice then. Let's tentatively plan on it. As a doctor, my life isn't my own while I'm at sea. Barring any emergencies, it should be fine."

"I've never been to Belize. It'll be nice to be with someone who knows the place."

That familiar pinging sensation bounced through her gut. "This is starting to sound like a date."

"Does it help to say it's my favorite part of this assignment so far?"

He ran his forefinger along her bottom lip, and she was shocked how that little bit of contact could make her knees go weak. Before she had a chance to recover from it, his mouth captured hers. The fleeting thought that he stole some of her toothpaste ran through her head before it was obliterated by the fireworks set off by a tongue that followed the path of his finger before entering her mouth.

She grabbed at his waist and held on, since his hands on either side of her head definitely weren't enough to keep her from collapsing at his feet. Then she whimpered in protest when he lifted his head and growled, "We are in so much trouble, Sage. You want me to ignore this thing between us, then I better not see you without a bra again. Pretending to be old friends is going to be hard enough."

He dropped his hands before stepping back. She collapsed into her chair, and he was gone before she could unscramble her brain enough to respond.

"I wasn't planning on having company. I planned to go to bed."

Chapter Seven

As she suspected, and hoped, her day so far wasn't nearly as busy as the one before. Dace kept Dr. Middleton and the nurses busy with drug tests on the crew. So much so, that if she hadn't known what was really going on, she would've been suspicious.

Dr. Middleton was just closing the door of the dispensary when she entered the hall and saw him pocket a prescription bottle before he turned to face her. His eyes darted to the side before they focused on her. He bobbed his blond head, then cleared his throat. "Hello, Dr. Brady."

A chill crept across her skin, giving her the weird feeling she was being watched by someone besides the doctor. Her gaze darted to the window on the door of the dispensary but she saw no one. Rolling her shoulders, she forced herself to relax. She didn't know Middleton very well, but she'd always liked him. Now he was looking at her funny. Not good.

Hoping to get a reaction that might give something away she decided to start a conversation. "Hello, Dr. Middleton. One of the crew having a serious problem?"

"Yes, actually. Sean Devlin. When he was spotting on the rock wall, a passenger fell on him and he sprained his wrist. I'm giving him some prescription ibuprofen for the pain so he doesn't have to miss work."

"Was he planning on coming back for it, because I just saw him leave the infirmary. I didn't notice his arm was bandaged, but he seemed in a hurry." Not. Since when had lying to her staff become part of her job description?

"Well, shoot," Middleton said, running a hand through his hair. "I thought he was going to wait for it."

"I'm headed up on deck. I can give it to him if I see him at the wall. If not, I'll have it delivered to his room."

He dug the bottle out of his pocket and held it out to her. "That would be terrific. Thanks."

Sage hoped the smile she gave him didn't come across as forced. If the doctor was the guilty party, she was playing with fire. If he was one of the good guys, and she didn't come across as normal, he might start wondering about her ability to handle the new position. And that was a slippery slope to losing respect for her authority.

"I'm just going to grab my medical bag. Here's hoping the passenger has nothing more serious than a muscle spasm, and that I find Sean. See you later, Doctor." She took a quick peek at the label on the bottle. Sean's name was on it. Looked like everything was on the up and up.

It wasn't until she was in the corridor outside the hospital that she let out a sigh of relief and relaxed her jaw muscles. She liked giving people the benefit of the doubt, so thinking Sean and Dr. Middleton might be working together to smuggle drugs merely because Sean had seen the doctor about an injury didn't feel right. She rubbed at the nagging ache in her temples. Still, she was rather proud of herself for intercepting the bottle so she could have a look at the pills to see if they were what Middleton claimed they were. As well as see how he reacted to her offer to pass them along for him. Which if she wasn't so paranoid, was perfectly normal.

As she made a quick detour to her cabin to check out the contents of the prescription bottle, she prayed the doctor didn't discover she'd made up the emergency that called her on deck. Sage didn't like being suspicious of everyone who touched the dispensary. Innocent until proven guilty, right? Most likely, Dr. Middleton was just as ignorant as she had been.

Heart beating only a tad faster than normal, she walked into the sitting area of her cabin, dropped her bag on the coffee table and set the bottle down next to it. After quickly extracting plastic gloves from her bag, she opened the bottle and shook the pills out into her hand. She only realized she'd been holding her breath when it escaped in a loud whoosh. White, oblong pills with the markings of hydrocodone.

Which could mean everything or nothing. Had he taken pills from the bottle of smuggled narcotics not knowing what was in there, or had he used that bottle on purpose because it was for his and Sean's personal use?

Hands shaking slightly, she returned the pills to the bottle, set it on the coffee table and slowly removed the gloves. If nothing else, her little maneuver had kept Sean from getting drugs he wasn't supposed to have. Unless, of course, Middleton meant for him to have the opioid because they were working together, helping each other support a drug habit. She took a deep breath.

Now what? She ran a hand around the back of her neck, suppressing the foreign desire to have a man there for moral support. Her father had done more than enough to make sure she never felt a need for that kind of help. From an early age, he'd forced her to stand on her own no matter how tough things got, never understanding a young child needed their parent to have their back. A five-year-old girl did *not* need to be forced to kill the poisonous spider in her bed.

But it was more than that. There was the comfort of having physical strength around in the face of danger, another thing she hadn't felt the need for in a long time. Her Judo skills made sure of that.

Money made people do crazy things. Drugs turned people into something they wouldn't normally be. Money and drugs? Not a combination she wanted to come up against. Ever.

As if she had a choice at this point. What had happened to quick thinking, calm in the face of catastrophe Sage? What the hell was she supposed to do now? Innocent or guilty, Dr. Middleton needed to believe she gave the prescription to Sean. But she couldn't give him hydrocodone when he was supposed to have ibuprofen. Unless they really were working together... *Damn it.* Then Sean would be expecting the hydrocodone to be in the bottle, and she could be putting herself in danger if she didn't give it to him. What a mess. Someone was guilty of murder, and if that someone was working with her and got one whiff she knew about the smuggling, she'd be next on the list.

Breathe. Take a minute, clear your head and *think.*

Several deep breaths later, she had a plan. Not much of one, but at least it would get her out of the jam she was in, without personally handing narcotics to an unsuspecting patient. Again. She grabbed her bag off the coffee table and headed back to the infirmary. As she entered the waiting area her heart hit her rib cage with a thump. Dace.

"Hello, Doctor Delicious. Did you forget about me?"

She suppressed a wince at the name. "I could never forget about you, Dace. Just got called out on a false alarm. Why don't you come on back, and we'll see how your arm is doing."

Without waiting for him to get up, she headed back to the exam room. It wasn't long before his body heat enveloped her from behind. Disturbing on one level and comforting on another.

She motioned to the exam table before walking over to the sink and washing her hands. "Have a seat. How are you feeling after working all day?"

She turned to face him as she dried her hands and leaned her hips against the sink. Just being in the same room as him calmed her. Heart rate settled, she pushed aside the personal perusal she wanted to give him and to look at him medically. He hid it well, but he was definitely exhausted and pale. Plus, she didn't like the flush in his cheeks. Unless it was because he was with her... *Stop it!*

He shrugged a shoulder and gave a grunt. She ran her eyes over his face again, trying to keep her expression neutral. He shouldn't look so worn out. He hadn't done much more than stand and talk to people all day. Nothing near the activity of a police detective on an average day. She turned away to gather the necessary supplies to change his bandage."I need to you to take off your shirt."

"Is that a personal request, or a professional one,

Dr. Watson?"

At the teasing in his voice she relaxed a bit and shot him a smile over her shoulder. She raised her brows. "Both?"

He chuckled and started unbuttoning his shirt. "Works for me."

Once she had everything laid out, she removed the dressing from his arm, keeping her eyes on the task by sheer force of will. If she dared glance beyond his well-toned bicep, she'd be done for. After fully exposing the wound, she bit the inside of her cheek. It wasn't healing as she would've liked. And why hadn't she called in Celeste to assist her? She needed his vitals and an extra pair of hands always came in handy. "I'm going to call Celeste in here to help with this. I should've done it right off."

"I'd rather you didn't."

That shook her. "Why?"

"The way you looked when you walked in the waiting room, I can tell something's up and I want to know what. We can't talk if she's here."

"All right, Sherlock. Something happened. But right now, I'm worried about you."

"Me?" An annoyed look crossed his face. "Why?"

"After two days, this"—she gestured to his injury—"should be doing better. It's not really worse, but it's no better. And you're not doing very well at hiding your exhaustion."

He gave a resigned sigh and let one hand fall to his side. "You're right. I shouldn't be so worn out after a day like today. I thought it was the pain getting to me. Ibuprofen merely takes the edge off."

"Which you knew would be the case from the get-go, and that could be part of it. The bigger issue, though, is the antibiotics. Have you been taking them?" She went to work on his arm, cleaning the wound, replacing the iodoform and re-bandaging it. To his credit he didn't flinch once.

"Honestly?"

She looked at him and raised her brow.

"Today is the first day I've taken one that's stayed down longer than five minutes."

With the new bandage securely in place, she turned away from him and pulled off her gloves, pitching them in the trash with more force than necessary. "You can put your shirt back on. I'm going to get your blood pressure and temperature." Which she should have done first. The close proximity to him was turning her brain to mush.

"You're still running a fever, and it's up a degree from the first time you came in." Bracing her fists on her hips, she gave him her best Dr. No-Nonsense glare. "You absolutely cannot afford to be stupid with this. Especially on a cruise ship with limited equipment and supplies, never mind visiting foreign countries where exposure to germs is higher. You need a shot of antibiotics right now. I'll have Celeste come in to do a CBC so I can check your white blood cell count. I want you back tomorrow for a repeat lab draw. Hopefully your count will be down because of the injected antibiotics. When Celeste is done, meet me in my office, please."

His glare belied the meek tone in his voice. "Whatever you say, Doc."

She turned at the door and tried not to smile. "By the way, that shot is gonna hurt like a mother but the antibiotic solution has lidocaine in it so that'll help. A bit."

****

Leaving Dace in Celeste's capable hands, Sage was relieved to have a few minutes to deal with the pills still burning a hole in her pocket. Hoping Dr. Middleton wouldn't be hard to locate, or busy with a patient, her palms broke out in a sweat when she found him in his office. Since when had talking with a colleague made her nervous? Since… Never.

She walked through his open door, set the bottle on his desk, and gave him what she hoped was a rueful smile. "My apologies, Doctor. I couldn't find Sean. Because I had to get back here for a scheduled appointment, I wasn't able to have them sent to his cabin, either."

He picked up the bottle from the desk and gave her a small smile that lit his brown eyes. "No problem. If he still wants them, he knows where to get them. Otherwise I'll just put them back in stock. Thanks for trying."

"You're welcome." She made a mental note to follow up on what happened and check the numbers on the fake bottle of ibuprofen to see if the pills came from there, as well as check them again later to see if they got put back. Then she decided it might help— everything—if she got to know him a little better. "Busy day?"

He leaned back in his chair, gestured for her to take a seat, and set his pen down on top of the papers he was working on. As she sat down, she let her breath out slowly. She hoped he didn't notice the blood pounding through her carotid. Doctors were trained to take note of such things. Should she try to casually cover it with her hand, or brazen it out and pretend her neck wasn't throbbing like crazy? Or maybe she should do something with her hands to draw his attention away from her face. This seriously sucked. The adrenaline junkie in her was past trying to uncover a cold-blooded killer.

"Not too bad. Injuries amongst the kitchen staff mostly. As I'm sure you well know. How about you? Settling into the new position okay?"

"Not yet, but getting there. I'm enjoying working with the passengers. It's a nice change. It's the boatload of paperwork—pun intended." She smiled, and hoped it covered the nerves. "That I'm not so thrilled with. It may be virtual, but charting is charting whether it's on a computer or in a paper file, as far as I'm concerned."

"Well, if we wanted to take care of paperwork for a living, we'd be doing an office job, wouldn't we?"

She chuckled. "Too true. How's the family? I'm sure it's hard to be away from them for so long at a time."

His expression clouded for a moment. "I miss them, but I'm grateful I'm allowed to have them on board with me during the summer when the kids are out of school. As soon as I'm a little better off financially, I want to start my own practice. Meanwhile, it's worth the sacrifice for all of us."

"This job definitely has its upside," she said. "And I guess we better get back to it. Sorry I couldn't get that scrip to Sean. I guess he'll have to come get it when he gets a chance. Now, however, I have to get to my office for a patient consult." She stood. "See you later."

"Good bye, Dr. Brady. And congratulations on the

promotion."

****

When Dace entered her office, Sage was already seated at her desk, and though on first glance it appeared she was busy with something, it didn't take much for him to realize she wasn't really doing anything. His fingers ached to smooth away the frown lines on her brow, and he didn't like the weariness in her body language.

He also didn't like how much it bothered him, or the way she got under his skin, or any of these new and disturbing feelings she roused in him. Since when had he cared so much about what a woman thought? Why did it bother him that *she* was the one taking care of him rather than vice versa? Throughout his career as a detective, he'd worked with several women who had his back, rescued him even. He'd never thought twice about it and was grateful for their skills. Their ability to give him what he needed in the moment was no different from a doctor helping him out when there was something physically wrong. Sage seeing him as vulnerable made him want to demonstrate how tough he was.

She wasn't some helpless female, or the victim of circumstance whom he usually dealt with. His desire to protect her was at an all-time high. Although the desire to protect was a requisite of the job, he relished helping those who couldn't help themselves. Was he subconsciously trying to make up for everything that went wrong with Donato by helping her? Was this more proof that Rocque was right to give him this assignment?

Shit. He swiped a hand down his face. He couldn't

think about this right now. He *hadn't* balked under pressure after Donato's death, he'd merely been distracted. It was just the effects of the infection in his wound that had him operating at less than one hundred percent right now. *That was all.* It was ridiculous of him to believe he could save everyone, every time.

She looked up and gave him a slight smile, her dark green eyes, the likes of which he'd never run across before, sent conflicting messages which had his heart rate rising instantly. Just a brief flash of desire and he was ready to shove everything off her desk, lay her on it, and get lost in her gloriousness. Which, considering how neat her desk was, she probably wouldn't appreciate. Her bathroom had been just as neatly arranged. She liked having things where they belonged.

Which didn't sit well either. He'd lusted after women before. Been hot and bothered, but never to the point he fought the desire to drop everything, *in that instant*, and satisfy his libido. And the nagging feeling that if he did it right here and now, it wouldn't be enough.

He dropped into the chair in front of her desk and forced himself to focus. So he looked at the diploma hanging on the wall above her head. Harvard. Wow. Okay, he was letting himself get distracted again. Something was up, and he needed to know what. How else could he protect her?

"What happened?"

She threw her pen on the desk and leaned back in her chair. He squeezed his eyes shut tight for a moment when she sank her teeth into her lower lip. *He* wanted to do that…

"I was playing spy."

Her disclosure was the shot of adrenaline he needed to get rid of his lethargy. "I told you not to mess with this, Sage. Leave it to me."

She narrowed her eyes and stiffened. "Since when did you become the boss of me?"

"I'm the cop here, remember? *I'm* the one who knows what he's doing. I bow to your expertise when it comes to anything medical, but you need to bow to mine when it comes to *drug smuggling.*"

She glared at him a few more moments before sighing in resignation. "You're right. I know it. It's my father's control issues raising their ugly head, so ignore it, okay?"

"Okay, I won't take it personally." He paused. "So, is it that *you* want to be in control, or is it that you don't like a *man* exerting control over you?"

Without looking at him, she picked up the pen and began doodling on a piece of paper. Clearly, he'd touched a nerve. Suddenly the pen stopped moving and she looked him in the eye. "I don't think it's information that's necessary for our ruse."

"It may not be something old friends would know about each other, but it's a good idea for me to know more about what's going on in your head. If we end up in a dicey situation, there could be dire consequences to one or both of us because we're reacting to each other rather than the situation at hand."

She blew out a breath and continued with the doodling, going over the same figure eight design repeatedly. "I was an only child; my mother died when I was little. I tried so hard to make my father proud of me, Dace. It wasn't until I started working here that I realized he's one of those people you can never please. Whenever he said jump, I asked, 'how high?' Now that I'm out from under that kind of control, I'm uber sensitive to it. My gut reaction is to balk whenever it feels like my father—or anyone—is trying to control me. One of the reasons I quit working in the ER—in the same hospital he ran—was because I learned he wasn't worthy of such devotion. So…"

She finally looked at him and gave him a half smile as she set the pen down. "Feel free to call me on it when I'm having an over-the-top-reaction to you telling me what to do." She leaned back in her chair. "Back to the problem at hand. I intercepted a prescription for ibuprofen which Dr. Middleton filled for Sean Devlin. I wanted to see the contents."

He sucked in air through his nose in an effort to center his thoughts. He needed to distance himself from this stupid paranoia about her safety. It was a smart move and might prove to be helpful in figuring out what was going on. "What did you find?"

"Hydrocodone." She ran her hands through her hair, mussing it a bit, and made him shift in his seat. "I didn't think beyond getting the bottle from him so I could check it. I freaked a little bit afterward and ended up giving it back to Middleton. Told him I didn't have a chance to give it to Sean and let him deal with it. In the end, I'm not sure we really learned anything. I thought he might be acting suspicious, but maybe it was me looking for things that weren't there. He's probably just as ignorant about this thing as I."

Though everything she said was true, his radar was going off in all directions. Not that she needed to know he had a gut feeling. It was more necessary for her to appreciate the need for caution. The escapade with the prescription bottle proved she may not.

"It may not seem like much, but it gives me an avenue to pursue. Do you know Sean very well?"

She looked at him silently, leaned forward and picked up her pen again, only this time started tapping it on the desktop. "Yes and no. I met him on my first cruise. I know a lot of the crew since my duties have been to treat their ailments and injuries. Sean and I haven't had the same schedule so there are months where I don't see him at all. He made a pass at me the first time I met him and was good-natured about my lack of interest. I'd say we're...friendly. I know him better than a lot of the other crew members, but we've never socialized."

She dropped the pen on the desk. Sudden realization dawned on her face. "Now that you've made me think about this, he *is* in here rather a lot. I'm going to have a look at his file." She reached for her laptop and repositioned it on the desk to open it.

"It could mean nothing, Sage," he told her while they waited for it to boot up. "In situations like this, all sorts of things start to look suspicious that really aren't."

"Maybe. But I have a feeling about this, Dace."

"And I'm sure your instinct is spot on in a medical situation. This is different. Don't let your imagination run wild is all I'm saying. I'm sure you could come up with a motive for most of the people who have access to the pharmacy."

"Whether it means anything or not, he's in here quite regularly for injuries which require pain killers. Hydrocodone mostly, though it is ibuprofen from time to time and the one from Dr. Middleton today, the ibuprofen, is in his record."

"You realize, of course," Dace reminded her, "with regular access to Mexican prescription drugs Sean doesn't need to go through the clinic to feed a habit?"

She frowned as she looked at him over the laptop. "Damn. Too true."

He watched her expression go from annoyed to '*aha*' and didn't like the way his stomach flipped with excitement.

"What about this, *Sherlock*?" she proposed, looking much too smug for his liking. "Going through the clinic and having a legitimate scrip doesn't negatively affect his random drug screens or pose a problem if his room is searched as part of regular procedure."

He nodded and couldn't stop the smile that spread across his face. She had some nice deductive skills, no matter how she applied them. "You're proving to be an excellent Dr. Watson. So, we're doing plan B tomorrow in Belize."

She narrowed her eyes. "Since when did *we* have a plan B?"

"Since you high-jacked that scrip." He stifled a grin. Time to get serious. He cleared his throat and his stomach did another little jig. He shifted in his seat and looked down at his hands in his lap for a moment. "We're doing more than spending the afternoon together tomorrow."

She sat up straighter. "That sounds like an order."

"It is. Though it wasn't my intention to make it sound that way. It's just that you're not going to like what we need to do, and I'm not sure the best way to put it."

"Spit it out, Dace. It's usually the best way."

"Theoretically." His eyes searched her face for a moment, though he had no clue what he was looking for. "We need to pretend a romantic interest in each other."

She pushed her chair away from the desk and shot out of it. "What the hell? You can't be serious. It's the absolute last thing I need to be doing with you. Things are complicated enough right now."

He stood, paced around the room once, then stopped in front of the desk and crossed his arms. "I know that. I don't like it any more than you do. A romantic involvement with someone you work with is a bad idea. And this physical thing between us will make it difficult to keep things professional."

"Tell me something I don't know."

"I've been thinking about this since we uncovered the drug smuggling, but there's no way around it. The position you're in is more dangerous now. It's not just about a murder in New Orleans. It's about drug smuggling going on right under your nose, and you're in the very job as Roberts when he got killed."

She sank back into her chair, the fight gone out of her. He sat too, leaned across the desk, and took her hands. They were ice cold. "I can't think of any other way to protect you that won't raise suspicion. The last thing we want is for the culprits to know for a fact you are on to them. Having a security guard for a boyfriend will make them think twice before trying anything during the cruise. It'll buy some time to figure out who it is without you becoming a bigger target."

She nodded once, then squeezed his hands before

pulling away. After several moments of silence, she asked, "What was plan A?

"We'd already planned on spending the afternoon together in Belize, plan A was pretending we're on a date."

"Okaaaay... So our comparing notes away from the ship has been scrapped. And plan B is?"

"Check out the pharmacies in Belize, see if they are a viable option for drug smuggling, maybe a little spying to see if we can catch someone from the ship purchasing anything. Basically, trying to find out if there's anything going on that I need to let my boss know about. And we can still compare notes if we need to, but as we're going to be pretending a romantic relationship, our getting together to do it on board won't look suspicious now. Another reason pretending we're a couple is a good idea."

When her eyes lit up, his breath caught in his chest. Did she actually like the idea of being his significant other? "Like a stake out?"

He was an idiot. In more ways than one, apparently. What was he thinking? If he put Sage in danger and... Donato bleeding to death flashed before his eyes.

Get a grip. He swiped a hand down his face. He could do this. Sage was an adult who'd handled all sorts of people and situations in a big city ER, not a vulnerable, inexperienced child. There was no reason she couldn't handle pretending they were on a date as they kept an eye on a few Belize pharmacies.

"Want me to check if Sean has time off tomorrow?"

He nodded and let himself smile just a tad as he

waited for her to check staff schedules for tomorrow. When he wasn't freaking out about something bad happening, he was excited about the idea of doing a little investigating with her. She had the skills for it. He wasn't averse to the idea of acting like her date either, which didn't bother him as much as it probably should.

"That would be helpful."

"He's got the day off," Sage said after flipping to another screen on the computer. "So maybe plan C? Follow him if he leaves the ship, and see if he hits any pharmacies or does anything else suspicious?"

He nodded his head, gave her a huge smile and a wink, and was excited about the next day for the first time in a long while. "We'll follow him a little bit, if he leaves the ship, when he first disembarks, but I don't want to waste a bunch of time trailing someone with no real reason for it. Our time would be better spent watching some pharmacies to see if there's anyone else who should be on my list of suspects."

"All right. I'll see if I can find out what Sean's plans are for tomorrow."

"Sage…"

She raised one hand in a sign of peace. "I'll be discreet. He won't suspect a thing."

He decided there was nothing wrong with getting a little vicarious enjoyment while they pretended to be a couple. Once the investigation was over, he liked the idea of dating her for real. Her face said she'd like that, too. Even if she was fighting the attraction. His instinct was spot on when it came to the opposite sex in that regard. "Maybe we can sneak in a little sightseeing too? It's my first time out of the United States. I'd like to spend a little time enjoying it."

God, he wanted to kiss her. More than he'd wanted to kiss anyone. Ever. So bad it had him wondering what would be the harm. Besides, they were pretending to be romantically involved so it was now part of the job.

Chapter Eight

Dace closed the cabin door behind him and pulled out his satellite phone, a faint smile still on his lips from his encounter with Sage. His assignment was proving to be more interesting than he initially thought. Most importantly, it now gave him the opportunity to prove to Rocque he *was* operating at one hundred percent. Well, once his arm quit bothering him so much. Even if he fought the urge to kiss Sage each time he looked at her. Them working together was temporary but the possibility of a real relationship once it was done, made it all easier. Gratification delayed and all that.

As he looked around his room, he sank to the end of his single bed. The room seriously sucked, it was so small and spartan. Especially after he'd seen Sage's quarters. He shrugged the feeling off. At least he didn't have to share like most of the crew. Though sharing with Sage wouldn't be bad…

Stop it! Dwelling on things like that only complicated the job he was here to do. And anything that made this assignment more difficult needed to be avoided. He couldn't afford to mess this up. Getting sexually involved with someone you worked in close proximity with was a big mistake he wasn't going to make again. Not if he was going to prove to Rocque he was as good as he ever was, that his personal demons weren't affecting his ability to do his job.

So having Sage fight her attraction to him was a good thing for now. Once he had a new assignment, however… He squeezed his eyes shut for a moment and took a deep cleansing breath. An emotional distraction had landed him the job of Cruise Ship Cop.

You're gun-shy Dace and I'm not working with you until you get your head on straight. Sorry, I'm going to Rocque with this.

He'd wanted to punch Sam Romero in the face at the time. He needed to work. It was all he had, all he was. If he couldn't be a detective, he wasn't anything. His partner was just being paranoid. He'd been distracted for a moment *that was all.* And nothing had gone wrong.

Except… There was that second time. When he was alone. The day Rocque had sent him home after Sam ratted him out. He'd been in his car, parked outside a convenience store, sure it was being robbed, and he'd done nothing. Nothing except sit there, feeling the beat of his heart pound relentlessly from the slash in his arm. Each throb a painful reminder of how he'd let Donato and his family down. He'd never know for sure if he really would've chickened out that day at the store, because nothing actually happened. He'd misread the situation. Which in itself was bad.

The next day, after Rocque told him he had to take a vacation, he'd been seriously pissed off. He was still pissed, but deep down he wasn't able to lose the niggling doubt he couldn't be trusted in a critical situation. Even so, he hadn't let up until Rocque gave him this assignment. If he messed this up, Rocque wouldn't give him another chance. To be perfectly honest, if he screwed up this time, he didn't deserve one.

He sighed and turned on his phone. After touching base with Rocque, he'd go to the cafeteria and eat with the crew. Maybe he'd overhear something important. Not everyone knew he was a security guard. They might let something slip. He placed the call to Rocque.

"Cap, it's Dace. Y'all have anything on those names yet?"

"How's the vacation going?"

He winced. God, he was such a pain in the ass sometimes. Not that he harbored the remotest desire to work for anyone else. "Having the time of my life. Taking a tour of Belize tomorrow afternoon. So, anything?"

"Most of the medical staff check out okay. John Middleton raises a red flag because his alibi is iffy, and he's carryin' a lot of debt. However, he has a family to support, as well as student loans to pay back, which is pretty normal in the circumstances. He would've benefited from the salary increase if he'd been given Dr. Roberts' position, so there's motive there."

Dace thought about that one for a second. "True. But with a family to take care of, he'd be risking a lot by murdering someone. Besides, most doctors want to save lives, not end them." He leaned over and squeezed the bridge of his nose. "All that debt is motive to get some easy extra cash. And if Roberts' found out and called him on it, you have motive for murder. It's certainly enough to keep my eye on him. What about Celeste Devereaux?"

"The fact she has access to the pharmacy is motive, I suppose, and as a nurse, she would certainly know how to kill someone to make it look like a heart attack, but she's clean, and, according to Captain Southerby, has an alibi."

Dace straightened in his chair, surprised at the relief he felt with the news. He'd only met Celeste a couple times, but he liked her. What Rocque told him proved his gut *was* working. "What about Roberts' nurse, Jack Henshaw?"

"Hmmm…" There was a shuffling of papers before Rocque continued. "Y'all might want to keep an eye on him. He doesn't have an alibi and is in the same position as Celeste. Easy access, and a way to make quick cash. Hard to imagine a nurse killing the doctor he works for, though—" He chuckled softly. "Although, according to my new squeeze who's a nurse it's not such a stretch."

"Will do. Anything else I should know?"

"That's all I've got, sorry. There's nothing new to report with the investigation here. Although with the discovery of narcotics being smuggled through the dispensary, it gives us reason to look into Roberts being murdered because of that."

"Okay. You also need to check out Caribbean Seas employee, Sean Devlin. He's not on the medical staff, but he's done some things lately that have me wondering. He's in the doctor's office a lot. Sage is suspicious of him, too, so he's worth a look."

"Sage, huh? How do you enjoy working with the lovely Dr. Brady? Certainly it makes up for getting this assignment, eh?"

After that crack, he certainly wasn't disclosing the pretense of them being lovers. Rocque didn't need any ammunition. "I'm not answering that. And for the record, this assignment still sucks. I'll let you know if I learn anything new after I get back from Belize."

He ended the call before his boss could torture him any further.

****

Sage took Dace to one of her favorite outdoor cafés in Belize City, glad that Sean Devlin chose to stop at the one directly across the street. Dace pulled out a chair for her, showing he had the manners of a southern gentleman, though he hadn't been raised in the South. Curiosity as to whether the South had rubbed off on him in more ways than his accent, or his parents trained him well, was quickly replaced with irritation. "I can't see anything if I sit here."

"Can't be helped. Sit down before you draw unwanted attention and I'll explain."

She did as he asked, though she hoped the look she gave him burned, or at least singed a bit. The second source for her irritation came after she had to wait until they ordered their drinks before he told her she couldn't look at anything besides the front of the café—and him.

"Though your sunglasses disguise you somewhat, it's a lot easier for Sean to recognize you than me, *chère*, even from across the street. All he's going to get is a view of you from behind. I, on the other hand, have my hat." He tugged on the bill of his baseball cap and pulled a pair of shades from his shirt pocket. "And glasses to hide who I am. The fact he hasn't seen me since the first day makes the odds of him noticing us go way down." The corner of his mouth quirked. "You'll have to make do with watching me for the duration."

Which did have its perks. She liked looking at the laugh lines around his eyes and mouth which said that although his job was serious, he still found a way to enjoy life. One corner of his mouth tilted up and his pale blue eyes shimmered like ice in the sun when something made him happy or struck him as funny. Now that she thought about it, she realized he smiled quite regularly since his injury started healing and the antibiotics had kicked in. She'd be happy watching him for a lot longer than the amount of time they'd be there eating. Then there was the fact she liked the way he'd randomly say *y'all* or call her *chère*. Pretending they were a couple could prove to be detrimental to her emotional health if she wasn't careful.

She was enjoying the sleuthing, too. More than she should considering the suspects were fellow-employees. Maybe it was because she had Dace with her today that made her feel safe. The idea of needing someone else to feel secure made her a little twitchy, but she liked it more than it bothered her. The mystery of it all made her eager to find out exactly what was going on. It was the same kind of thrill she got coming up with a diagnosis for a patient. Figuring out the problem, then finding a solution. She liked being a problem-solver, though she preferred solving problems that involved helping someone. Delving into the dark side of people's lives was not very appealing—which led her back to wondering why she was happy to be part of this investigation.

Did her father's addiction to prescription drugs have something to do with her desire to expose the person using the dispensary to facilitate their own, or someone else's habit? The bite of her nails into her palms warned her to relax. Bottom line, it was *her* department, and it could be one of her staff members who was abusing her trust or one of the crew playing them all for fools.

She hoped it wasn't Sean; at the same time she wanted it to be him, because it meant she wouldn't have to suspect her good friend, Eric Roberts. Dace's sigh brought her back to the here and now. "I'm starting to wonder if following Sean is a waste of time. He hasn't done anything suspicious. I'm thinking, once we've eaten, we should hunt up some pharmacies and see if anything happens there." He held the menu up in front of him and started perusing it. "I can't believe I'm saying this, but right now I kind of wish I really was on vacation, and we could spend the afternoon exploring the city."

"The next time we're here with time off, I can show you around. Maybe go to the Mayan ruins. Or we could go snorkeling at Ambergris Caye. If you end up working on the ship longer than this one cruise that is."

"If we bail on the investigation, do we have enough time for something like that today?"

"You're starting to make me wonder what kind of cop you are."

He gave her a faint smile. "Ignore me. I'm feeling rather frustrated being in this exotic place and not *doing* anything exotic. Makes me think I should've taken the vacation time after all. Which is insane."

"You could order an exotic drink, or something off the menu that's local rather than tourist-y."

He sighed again, rather dramatically she thought, though the slump of his shoulders worried her a bit. Maybe he wasn't recovering as quickly as she'd first thought. "It'll have to do. What do you recommend?"

"Depends. Are we talking local-favorite, or tourist-favorite Belize fare?"

"Definitely local. I've enjoyed a variety of rather strange Southern dishes in New Orleans in the last several years. Like raccoon baked with sweet potatoes. If I remember correctly, Belize has a bit of a Creole influence."

Surprised he knew such details about food, she nodded. "It does. I'm thinking you should try the Gibnut stew with rice and beans." She made an effort to come across enthusiastic about the dish, but had a hard time suppressing a smile.

"Gibnut stew it is then." He set his menu on the table. "Okay, the expression on your face has me worried."

"Pretty sure it's nothing like what you've had in Louisiana, though maybe similar meat. It's a rainforest rodent. Still game?"

"Oh definitely. Bring it on. There's hot sauce on the table, so I can always douse it in that if it's too gamey."

Now she had something else to admire about the man: his adventurous spirit. Her glance rested on his wide mouth for a moment, the full bottom lip, and that endearing hint of a smile. She seriously needed to work harder to ignore such things. They led nowhere good.

She had yet to be brave enough to order anything as strange as rainforest rodent, though she ordered Ceviche, a Belize specialty, which was cool and refreshing now the day was starting to get warm. As the waiter set their food in front of them, she had an overwhelming urge to get to know everything about him, no matter how boring. "Though you come across as a bit of a Southern boy, you mentioned you grew up on Lake Michigan. Where exactly?"

"Holland, Michigan. A small town on Lake Michigan, though I moved to Chicago not long after I graduated college."

"I know Holland. As cold as Chicago is in the winter, since it's on the lake. How did you end up living so far from home in New Orleans? Tired of the cold?"

He shook his head and narrowed his eyes. She frowned down at her plate before scooping up a bite Ceviche with a tortilla chip. She forced herself to ignore how much his reluctance to answer bothered her.

"A buddy of mine and I came down to help with disaster relief after a hurricane. I helped with rebuilding structures, as well as in law enforcement for about a year, and decided to stay because it was a place I felt I could make a difference. So I got a permanent job on the NOPD."

Her stomach sank even as her heart soared. This wasn't some cop on a power trip or a detective who got his ego stroked every time he solved a case. This was a man who genuinely wanted to protect and serve. This was a man who could creep into her heart and change her forever. She shifted in her seat, the creaking of the rattan chair easily heard over the sound of a passing car.

"Don't look at me like that." He scowled and jabbed a piece of food onto his fork. "I knew I should've just said I needed a change."

She shook her head, looked down at her plate and pushed her food around with her fork. "No, no, it's not that, though I do admire your motives."

Her gaze traveled to his empty plate before looking back at him as he chewed his last bite of gourmet rodent. She couldn't help but appreciate the fact he'd enjoyed something so out of the ordinary. Like she needed anything else to admire about the man. She was way out of her comfort zone as it was. It felt like they truly were friends. How had that happened so quickly? She just about jumped out of her skin when he sat up straight and pulled out his phone.

"I want you to pose for me like I'm taking your picture, but I'm going to be taking several of our suspect. He looks like he's up to something after all."

Sage quickly set down her fork. She didn't like the way he referred to Sean as a suspect, even if it was technically correct. She started to turn around to see what he was talking about.

"Hell, *chère*, don't try to look, you can see the pics later. C'mon, I don't want to miss this. Pose. *Now*."

He may not be taking pictures of her, but she did her best to look good for the camera—just in case. If a picture of her inadvertently ended up on his phone, she wanted it to be a good one. More fool her. Focusing on that made it easier to resist the urge to turn around and see for herself what was going on. When she was finally able to look through the pictures, she realized Dace not only had a seriously good camera on his phone, but also had photography skills. She shivered despite the heat of the Belize sun. Seeing pictures of Sean making a drug deal as though it was something out of a movie brought the reality of the situation home like a blow to the stomach, doubled over with pain and gasping for air. A drug smuggler and murderer on board the ship was no longer an intangible someone. He had a face. He was a real person.

Sean can't seriously be the guy. It went against everything she knew about the man. Still, it had happened right under their noses just now. She swallowed. Not only to find her voice, but to neutralize her feelings. "These pictures are good. You've done this before. Obviously that waiter is passing something to Sean, and you even managed to get a photo of it. Is that really a package of cocaine?" She groaned. "I *like* Sean."

He took the phone back. "Most likely it's coke. In any case, I'm recording the name of the restaurant on my phone so I can give it to my boss." He quickly logged in the information, then shifted in his seat as he put it back in his pocket. "Sean's got that skinny, drug-addict look to him, so it could be he's involved in trafficking to feed a habit, rather than for the money. Not that the way he looks in itself is anything, but now I've seen him dealing drugs. And addicts are more apt to do something they normally wouldn't to feed their habit. Or hide it. Like murder. It's not looking good at the moment."

"I guess, since I'm not a police officer, I don't instantly jump to that conclusion with every skinny person I meet. There's plenty of explanations for it, genetics for instance."

"Sorry, I wasn't questioning your skills or writing Sean off as a drug addict just because of how he looks. It's my job to be suspicious and yours to look at all the possibilities. I'm not going to ignore what we just saw either, though. What I have now is enough for me to put Sean at the top of my list of suspects, as well as a good reason to keep a closer eye on him. Starting with shaking down his room. Whether or not he's connected with prescription drug smuggling or murder, based on what I just saw, he's involved in some serious shit."

She nodded in agreement though she didn't like it. She thought of herself as a good judge of character. Never in a million years would she have suspected Sean of smuggling drugs. Maybe everything that happened in Chicago put her off her game more than she realized. "So it appears we've stumbled upon even more mess than you expected when you took this assignment."

He smiled and she momentarily forgot what they were talking about. She could spend the rest of her life enjoying that look on his face. Twice in a matter of minutes Dace had conjured emotions in her that were new. It set her on edge.

"It's now time for plan D. Hope you feel like dessert and coffee."

"Uh…"

"By the way, Sean's leaving, but we're not going to follow him. If you'd like you can move seats and watch what's going on across the way with me."

"Heck yeah." She shifted into the chair next to him. "So that's plan D?"

He nodded. "I want to keep an eye on that waiter, and see if anyone else from the crew shows up. You may recognize them easier than I. It was a good-sized package being transferred, so most likely it's being smuggled in order to be sold rather than for personal use. I'd like to know if there's anyone else from our ship doing the same thing."

"So this takes priority over finding out if any of the crew are smuggling opioids?"

"For the moment."

"Tell me why you, a police detective, are sniffing out drug traffickers? Doesn't the DEA have that sort of thing covered?"

He ran a hand around the back of his neck and blew out a breath. Before he could answer, the waiter stopped at their table to ask if they needed anything else. After placing an order for dessert and iced coffee, he answered. "Well, yeah… It's complicated." The hand that rested on the table clenched, and a muscle in his jaw twitched as he turned away from her and focused on what was happening at the café across the street.

She knew he was struggling but was oddly hurt by his reluctance to talk. Really, why did she care so much about what happened to put him on this assignment? Or exactly what that assignment involved? She wasn't part of the case. She was merely supposed to give him any information he might need. And act like they were old friends. Scratch that. Now they were supposed to be romantically involved. "Hey, if it's necessary for you to keep that a secret, forget I said anything. It's none of my business what your job entails. It's really none of my business if it's personal either. Unless it may affect your health in some way."

He pulled his ball cap off and threw it on the table before ruffling his fingers through his hair. The words that came out of his mouth, though not louder than anyone else talking around them, were violent and crude. The emotion driving them was enough to dissipate any anger and hurt. Whatever it was he wasn't telling her, impacted him, big time.

"The truth is, I screwed up and an innocent person, a person I was supposed to protect, got killed. Technically, I wasn't held responsible. On paper, I was just doing my job. But I was so obsessed with catching the bad guy, I lost sight of who might get in the way of

129

that. A—child got killed before I could take the bastard down."

"And this relates to the assignment you're doing now, how?"

He looked away from her, a muscle twitching in his jaw. When he returned his attention to her, the expression on his face was enigmatic. "Since we're working together, I suppose you have a right to know. I certainly expected the same kind of information from you. The powers that be feel my head is too messed up to do my job properly. I was ordered to take time off or take this assignment with the cruise line." He not only made air quotes around the word 'job' but spat it out like it tasted foul. "Personally, I think they made it up for me, not realizing it would turn into a real case. So, I don't have the authority right now to do anything to these people who are committing crimes, other than turn them in, along with any information I uncover about drug smuggling, or Dr. Roberts' death.

"As for the DEA… Yeah, they're the ones who need to know about what we've seen today. But the more I can learn about this, if my information leads to some big arrests, then I can prove to Rocque I'm as good at my job as I ever was. That I'm not some sort of mental case because of what happened to Donato."

She raised her brows when he called the child by his name but didn't call him on it. So it was personal. He'd given away more than he probably realized, and it explained why he was having such a hard time. "Why do you think it was your fault, Dace?"

The shutters came down and his expression hardened. He sat up straight in his chair, scrambling in his pocket to pull out his cell phone. "Our waiter is a busy fellow. Do you know the person he's dealing with now?"

Ignoring how her heart sank to her toes when she realized he wasn't going to confide in her anymore about what happened, she did her best to appear nonchalant as she turned to look at the situation. She located the waiter from Dace's pictures and checked out the person he was serving. "He doesn't look familiar to me. Sorry."

"Hey, not your fault. We'll hang here for another half hour or so, see if we happen to catch anyone from the ship. Belize is a favorite for drug traffickers, so it certainly wouldn't surprise me if there were others from our ship involved in this. After that, let's check out some pharmacies, and see what they have to offer anyone in the market for smuggling prescription drugs. Maybe we can see something going down there."

****

It worried him. The way just looking at her made him feel. Turned on, protective, insecure, *jealous.* She'd made it clear, more than once, she wasn't interested romantically in Sean. Yet, all she had to do was say she liked him and act upset that he could be a drug addict, and Dace's gut twisted, he felt his blood pressure rise, and instantly wanted to run hell bent for leather across the street and strangle the guy. Then he'd catch a glimpse of fear or pain in her dark green eyes, and he was consumed with a need to pull her close, hold her head to his chest and soothe it all away. What was wrong with him? This assignment was supposed to give him time to get his head straight, but with each day that passed the more muddled it became.

After a visit to the pharmacy, they discovered

prescription drugs were too pricey in Belize to make them worth smuggling across the border for a profit. Mexico was the place to pick them up at a cost that made smuggling worthwhile, something he would've asked Rocque about if he wasn't so distracted by Dr. Delicious.

"It's irritating we're no closer to figuring out what's going on with the drugs in the dispensary. Your job must get pretty frustrating at times, Dace, chasing down leads that don't pan out."

He shrugged. "The thrill that the next thing might be the answer I'm looking for outweighs the letdown of a dead end. Besides, we have accomplished something today. We learned one of the many sources of drug trafficking in Belize. It's good intel."

What he wanted more than good intel, was to know exactly what was going on, because discovering that would put Sage out of harm's way. His stomach burned every time he thought about her being caught in the middle of anything involving illegal drugs.

"What would you like to do now?" she asked. "We still have a couple hours."

Seeing Dr. Brady in a bikini popped into his head. Maybe a little break to enjoy being a tourist would be good for him. "Swimming, maybe. Or a museum, if you'd rather get out of the sun."

She kept her gaze on the water when she spoke. "I hope you're not married to the idea of swimming, Detective Langdon."

Uh oh… That was her doctor voice. He raised his brows.

"Have you forgotten about your injury? The last thing you're going to want is salt water on it. And I've nothing with me to replace your bandage if it gets wet."

Hell yes, he'd forgotten. "Museum it is then. Have you been?"

"Actually, I haven't. There's Mayan ruins not far from here, and I know the museum has a lot of Mayan artifacts. I keep telling myself that one of these times I'm going to check them out. I'm not much of a history buff, so I tend to get lured into more of the sightseeing or the physical-type things the area has to offer when I'm here. Museum it is, and it's not much of a walk."

"If you know where you're going, lead the way."

"You're going to like this, I think."

"What makes you think the museum will appeal to me?"

"The building used to be the jail. In fact, they've turned one of the jail cells into an exhibit."

He chuckled. "Since I'm a police detective, you think touring an old prison would appeal to me?"

She threw him a careless smile. "Pretty much."

His heart pounded harder for a few beats. Over a simple smile. *Damn...* His laugh didn't sound as light as he hoped. "You're right. Now I can't wait to see it."

His first glimpse at a third world country was disturbing. He didn't want to think of how many people all over the world lived in similar conditions. Not that New Orleans didn't have its share of beggars and poor living conditions, but the opportunities to live a better life were much harder to come by here. He understood the temptation for some to get involved in drug trafficking. The whole situation had him on high alert. In a place like this, things could get ugly before you realized what was happening.

Chapter Nine

The museum had a towering stucco wall topped with a black wrought iron fence running its length. As they walked along next to it, the hairs on the back of Sage's neck stood on end. She could've sworn they were being watched.

She took a quick peek over her shoulder. A flash out of the corner of her eye had her muscles tensing, until she heard the meow of a cat. Geez. They were being stalked by a cat, and she was freaking out. She shook her head and rolled her shoulders, trying to make the creepy sensations go away, but it didn't work. She glanced across the street, looking for anything that would put her mind to rest, but there was no one. Anywhere. No tourists wandering around, no locals, much less anyone she recognized from the ship. Well, it was siesta time…

The scuff of a shoe that wasn't hers or Dace's, convinced her someone was there, so she checked over her other shoulder. Nothing. She wondered how Dace could be walking along next her not noticing any of it. He was the detective here. Why wasn't he detecting?

She looked up at him and his expression told her nothing and his relaxed body language screamed carefree tourist taking in the sights. His hands shoved in his pockets, baseball cap pushed back on his head, sunglasses in place. The only thing missing from the picture of complete nonchalance was whistling under his breath.

Was this investigation making her paranoid now? Sensing danger when nothing pointed to it. She sighed in disgust. She shouldn't be worried. She was trained to handle herself in dangerous medical situations. Plus, she was with an experienced police officer who'd faced more danger and came out intact, than she ever had or ever would.

By the time they reached the entrance to the museum, where the wall was higher and had bricks imbedded in it to form an arch over the wrought iron gate of the entryway, the pep talk hadn't helped. She couldn't shake the feeling someone was watching them, and couldn't convince herself it was because of Belize City's reputation. She'd visited it numerous times and never worried about danger. Maybe it was because there was no one around so she felt like they were on their own if anything went wrong. The security guard standing on the sidewalk at the entrance to the museum eased her fear and she felt her muscles relax when she saw him.

Inside the coolness of the building, surrounded by artifacts from ancient peoples and civilizations, she gained perspective, as well as her calm. The world was so much bigger than her and the things she was dealing with right now. She savored the opportunity to escape it all here. In the company of a man like Dace. For the first time in far too many years, she let everything go and enjoyed an afternoon with a man she was attracted to on a variety of levels. And if her instincts were to be believed—though she'd been questioning them lately—he was enjoying it too. Still, as they paused in front an impressive display of carved Mayan jade, she couldn't fight the overwhelming need to ask him the question that had been bugging her since day one.

"Dace, how did you get knifed?"

He tensed—no surprise there—and muttered a foul word under his breath. That didn't surprise her either. As far as she was concerned, the question needed to be asked. For more than just curiosity's sake. He turned away from the display to look at her and there was a long silence. She began to wonder if he was going to answer. Which, for her, would be an answer in itself about pursuing any kind of relationship with him when they were no longer working together. She didn't want to get involved with a man who wasn't willing to talk with her about hard stuff. And without a doubt, this was some hard stuff for Dace. She shook her head at herself. Just because it felt like she'd known him forever, felt comfortable enough around him to talk about her father, didn't mean it was the same for him. It had only been a few days. She was probably expecting too much. And really, was she seriously considering getting into a relationship with any man?

She turned from the display, ready to tell him he didn't have to answer, to apologize even, but the words died on her lips. Her gaze was snagged by his intense regard, so many emotions swirled in those eyes, she could hardly grasp them all.

Except for the pain, which came across loud and clear.

"My boss thinks I can't handle my job because of what happened that night."

He sighed and squeezed his eyes shut for a moment. The look on his face when he opened them made her blood run cold. *What the hell had happened that could be worse than a child dying?* Maybe it was too big of a question to be asked in a museum.

He grabbed her arm and escorted her to a nearby bench. Out of the way of the few visitors making their way through the museum with them. After they were seated, he scrubbed his hands down his face, looked at her for a moment, then looked back at the jade display. Right as she was about to tell him he didn't have to answer, he spoke. "Donato was a good kid living in a horrible situation."

"Donato?"

She held her breath, wondering if he was going to say more. Maybe he needed to pretend she wasn't there to get the words out. "My...informant, for want of a better word. He was thirteen, his mother worked two jobs just to keep the family afloat because his father wasn't around. His older brother, Demetrius, was out of school, involved in a gang and dealing drugs. He also had a little sister. Amelia's five."

He looked down at his hands as though all the answers were there and instantly stopped wringing them. She reached over and placed a hand on top of both fists. The doctor inside wanted to make it better. To her surprise, he didn't pull away, instead he turned one of his hands over and wrapped his fingers around hers.

"Donato was at the age where most boys in his neighborhood start joining gangs. I met him while I was doing an investigation in his neighborhood and he kinda latched onto me. He'd call me at the station whenever he had some information he thought I could use. Demetrius, his older brother, wanted him to join his gang, but Donato told me he would never do it. He wanted to be a cop. He wanted to fix things, to make them better for his mom and little sister. He came to the police station one day and insisted on being my informant, even though I made it very clear it was a really lousy idea. He ignored me and started passing along more detailed information which he thought might be helpful, and indeed it was. Then one day he announced he was going to pretend he was interested in becoming part of his brother's gang. He thought it would help make his dream of getting rid of the gang activity in his neighborhood a reality, if he could supply inside information. And if all it took was conviction and determination, there's no question he would've made it happen." He dropped her hand and swiped his down his face. "*God*!"

He looked at the floor for a moment, then up at a display across the room. She doubted he saw anything but the scene in his head. Every muscle was tensed, like he was ready to fight. Fighting his feelings maybe? She longed to wrap her arms around him and tell him it was going to be okay. To somehow magically make his emotional pain disappear as easily as giving a patient morphine makes physical pain go away.

He barked out a harsh laugh. "I let a thirteen year old kid talk me into doing something I knew was inappropriate. He was a very determined little punk. He would've made a difference in this world, I know it." He closed his eyes briefly. "It's my fault he can't."

She doubted that. No one can control the actions of another person. Her father had given it a damned good try, and she was living proof it didn't work.

"How is it your fault, Dace?"

"I should never have given in and let him be my informant. He was a kid. And he never had a chance to really be one.*"*

What he was saying made her heart literally hurt. *Was that possible?* She ached for Dace. For Donato. For his mother and sister even.

"Dace, you know the only person we can control is ourselves. If he was as determined as you say he was, Donato was going to do what he was going to do. At least he had you to keep an eye on him while he was doing it. It wasn't your fault." The expression on his face told her he wasn't buying it, and though she didn't want to argue about it, not now, it needed to be said. "Tell me what happened. It will make you feel better to talk about it."

"I *have* talked about it. To my boss, Rocque, and I've told the story what feels like a million times verbally and on paper. It's changed nothing."

"A run-down of events for a police report isn't talking about it, Dace. Talking about how it made you feel is what's going to help you move on. Dealing with your feelings and having someone give you the proper perspective on those. Your boss making you take this job of security officer is his way of trying to get you to deal with it."

"You too now, huh?"

She bristled. She was trying to help him, why couldn't he see that? She stifled the desire to make a sarcastic retort, because that definitely would *not* help. "I am a medical professional who might know something about the subject. Your captain was on the right track, and probably knows you well enough to have a handle on what works with you. Ordering you to see a therapist would most likely make the situation worse."

"So you think you know what I need now too?" He clenched, then unclenched his jaw so hard she saw the muscles move, heard the grinding of his teeth. "Donato woke me with a text saying he'd followed his brother to the gang leader's house, was sitting underneath an open window, listening to them talk. It was two in the morning, for Christ's sake! No kid deserves a parent so worn out from life they don't know their son is traipsing around a bad part of New Orleans at two in the morning. I told him to go home and go to bed. That I would take care of it."

"He didn't, did he?"

He shook his head. "I think he wanted to get these guys off the streets worse than I did. And he was scared for his brother. And tired of the bloodshed. The kid was barely a teenager and had seen more people die than anyone should at any age." He shook his head. "It's not right."

Didn't she know it? Hadn't she seen it firsthand in Chicago? Life in the inner-city was tough on anyone who came in contact with it, much less those who lived with it day in and day out. It seemed as though her heart was being squeezed by a fist and her blood had stopped pumping at a normal rate from the pressure on it.

"No, it's not. And I admire men like you who tackle it head-on on a daily basis."

"Yeah, well…"

He shrugged, and some of the tension drained from him with the action. He turned toward her, moving slightly away to rest his arm along the back of the bench. The expression in his eyes wasn't as icy.

Talking about it like this, not like it was some police report to get the facts, was working. She let her breath out slowly, careful not give away how desperate she was for him to tell her all of it so she could help him move on with his life. She wanted him to be able to heal, and the strength of that desire was a little unnerving.

"It's all about turf wars and getting even with rival gangs, and that night his brother's gang was going to get even. Lives were at stake, and this time Demetrius's was too. Donato texted me where they were headed, and I told him again to go home, that I'd handle it from there. I let my partner know what was going on, then went to see if Donato was right. I figured as soon as I knew for sure if there was trouble brewing, I'd get the department's asses down there. And to put it mildly, it got ugly. Donato got killed."

His pale eyes bored into hers as the silence dragged on, and the ice in his gaze made a chill dance across her skin despite the heat in the room. Her stomach clenched when he scrubbed a hand down his face, only then realizing how much he'd said.

Her words came out in a whisper. "How did he get killed?"

He shook his head and stood up, the expression on his face decidedly blank as he held his hand out to her. "I'm not talking any more about this here. You've got the gist of what went down. And like I told you, I've talked about it already. It doesn't help. Besides, it's time we headed back to the ship before it leaves without us."

She mentally shook her head, trying to adjust to the sudden change of subject, and the change in him, as she

141

took his hand and stood up. "Sure."

He let go of her hand as they started moving toward the exit of the museum, and she desperately tried to convince herself it didn't matter. He hadn't meant anything by it.

After they stepped out onto the street and headed away from the museum, she took a moment to rein in emotions that ranged all over the place. The strongest one being distress over the power this man held over those emotions. They were about halfway down the sidewalk before the other feeling, the one she'd been trying to ignore earlier, returned. The one that said she was being watched, that danger was lurking close by. She rotated her neck to get rid of the sensation and could hardly wait until they were back in New Orleans, where she didn't have to think about Dace, drug smuggling, or murder.

Then she realized, once again, she should've listened to her instincts.

****

Two things happened real fast. His stomach went down like the Titanic then his ears started ringing.

Damn it. Caught up in the recent past, he'd failed to pay attention to their surroundings, or that Sage was walking a few paces ahead of him. Stupid, rookie mistake. He'd known they were being followed on the way to the museum. Epically bad decision to tell Sage about Donato just because she'd asked. It took his head out of the game.

Now she was being threatened with a weapon, commanded to hand over her purse, and what does she do? Hitches up the purse higher on one shoulder so it rested on her back, making it harder for the guy to grab.

"Hell, no. I work with knives for a living, yours doesn't scare me."

"Have you lost your mind, Sage? For Christ's sake, give him the damn purse."

"Listen to the man, bitch," the punk said. "Give over the purse. I'll take your wallet too, *Hombre*."

Eyes hard with determination, Sage looked over at him, and his blood curdled. In that moment he knew she wasn't going to hand over her purse, and something was seriously wrong in his universe because, rather than catapulting him into action, this scenario conjured up his last moments with Donato.

Get the hell out kid! Get safe and let me do my job.

But Donato didn't listen and that asshole grabbed him and held a knife to his throat. Then, when Dace tried to save him…

He shook his head to clear it. No way in hell something like that was going to happen again on his watch. *Get your shit together, Langdon.*

Sage caught them both by surprise. With a swift kick, the knife clattered to the ground. Blood spurting from his nose, the thug landed on his stomach before either of them had a chance to realize what she was up to.

Hot damn. Watching her do that shouldn't turn him on, but at least his brain hadn't completely turned to mush. The man started to scramble to his feet but Dace kicked him in the back, hard. He went back down to the pavement before he could catch himself with his hands. Dace followed him with a knee on his spine and twisted his arm up between his shoulder blades. He winced when his own injury made itself known.

"You picked the wrong targets today, *Hombre*." He

looked over his shoulder at Sage who stood there with a satisfied look on her face. He resisted the urge to smile at her. Things could've been very different if she hadn't known how to handle herself.

"Go back to the museum and have the security guard call the authorities." He let out a frustrated growl when it struck him again how badly things could've gone wrong. "Don't you know you're supposed to give anyone who pulls a weapon on you whatever they ask for?"

"I can take care of myself, Detective. It's not the first time I've had a knife pulled on me. I learned Judo for that very reason."

He shook his head and turned his attention back to his captive. *This time* the bad guy wasn't getting away. His arm throbbed mercilessly. Dammit! As he waited for back-up to arrive Dace saw a thin trail of blood creep down his arm.

Dr. Brady isn't going to like this.

Chapter Ten

Sage stretched out flat on her bed, trying to decide if it was worth the effort to get something to eat. It had been a long time since lunch, but a lot had happened today, and she was emotionally and physically drained.

Then there was the more insidious appetite. One that involved a man she was pretending to have a relationship with. She couldn't stop herself imagining him lying on his bed, his shirt stripped off, pants begging to be removed. It was the first time in quite a while she'd been tempted to wind down the way she once did after a stressful shift in the ER.

And the first time ever someone as delicious as Dace was available. But she was determined not to indulge herself in old behaviors.

Right now was not the best time for Dace to enter her orbit. She was so close to getting her life together, and somewhere along the way she'd decided she was done hiding from everything by sailing around the Caribbean and playing at being a doctor. The loss of Eric, the events of the last few days, maybe even spending so much time with Dace, had helped her realize she wanted to tackle life on dry land again.

Maybe not the stress of working in an ER, but certainly in a hospital where she made a difference in people's lives. One of the things she'd liked about working in an ER was being there for people who desperately needed medical help. Working in a low-income clinic could bring the same kind of satisfaction. Who knows, maybe simply not working for her father would make the stress of working in an ER manageable.

She had to admit she might have gone overboard by trying to get away from the person she was when she left Chicago. Did she really plan on never having sex again just because she'd had it for all the wrong reasons during her twenties? Had she created another problem when she escaped to reinvent herself? Or was she looking for justification to act on this primal desire for one Dace Langdon?

It wasn't as though there'd been no opportunity to get involved with someone until now. Cruise ships had their fair share of young, attractive people working on staff and she'd met several men who would've appealed only a few years ago. Men like Sean, who'd wanted to capture her interest but couldn't. What was it about Dace who made her long for things she once enjoyed, but also those she'd never realized she wanted? Watching him pin that thug to the ground made her want him so badly, in a way that went beyond physical, it became hard to breathe. There was something about a man using his physical strength to defend a woman… Merely thinking about it now made her heart thunder in her chest.

One thing she did know for sure. Between his control issues and drug addiction, her father did a real number on her. Here she was, after a decade of being out from under his roof, with her head still a mess.

Dace probably wasn't the only one who could benefit from a little talk therapy.

Maybe it was because she'd never talked with anyone about her father. She was pretty sure telling Eric Roberts she'd left Chicago because her and her father couldn't see eye to eye didn't count. He'd never pressured her to say any more, silently gave her a shoulder to cry on and never mentioned it again. Then, he'd helped her in more subtle ways: commending her, giving her responsibility, trusting her to take care of the staff instead of always looking over her shoulder the way her father had.

Her stomach did a little dance when a knock sounded on the cabin door. Right now, she wanted to see Dace so badly, she immediately assumed it was him. Not that she trusted herself to be around him right now, and when she remembered the look in his eyes when he'd pinned that creep to the ground...

He'd wanted her as much as she wanted him. She was pretty sure she didn't have the strength to fight them both.

It was Dace standing there, holding two paper bags, the smell of hot, fried chicken wafting around him. Groaning in defeat, she swung the door wide, moving to one side so he could enter. "Get your fine ass in here detective. I am so hungry, you have no idea."

"Hell, *chère*, any more talk like that and we'll be satisfying a different hunger altogether and eating this when it's cold."

She followed him to the sitting area considering how tempting it may be to watch Dace's tight glutes and realizing how she'd used sex merely to feel good in the moment, as a way to escape reality rather than to connect emotionally and spiritually with another human. It helped fortify the determination she wasn't going to be that woman. Ever again.

She squeezed her eyes shut and let her breath out slowly in an effort to suppress her longings and regain a modicum of control. She could enjoy a meal with the man, spend time with him, and be content. She didn't need to take it any further just because sexual tension vibrated like a snare drum. She wanted to get to know him better before anything sexual happened. She'd enjoyed talking with him over lunch. She liked the connection they'd made over the last few days and wanted to build on that before she considered anything more.

That was, if *he* liked *her* enough to make it anything more than sexual. So, now was the time to figure that stuff out. Not after they'd slept together.

She sat at the small dining table while he unpacked the food. Had he gone back ashore for fried chicken? Too hungry to care, she didn't say anything until he finished unloading the bags, sat down across from her and they'd taken the edge off their hunger with a few bites.

"Thanks for bringing dinner. You take good care of me."

Dace licked a piece of chicken off his bottom lip and looked at her across the table. "I could've taken care of that guy this afternoon. You should've let me handle it. I'm trained for situations like that. You might have ended up losing more than your purse, maybe been seriously injured or killed."

It was so out of the blue, she blinked twice, then tried to figure out the best way to respond without treading all over his ego. "I didn't really think about it at the time. Once in the ER, I was caught unaware by a man who was high as a kite. It was a lesson well-learned so I got training on what to do if it ever happened again. As I demonstrated on that sorry excuse for a man today." She shrugged. "All's well that ends well."

Dace, on the other hand… She'd bet his objection had less to do with her ability to handle being attacked, and more to do with how badly he was dealing with Donato's death. Was he ever going to appreciate the benefit of expressing his feelings about what happened? She wanted to hit him upside the head, knocking some sense into him. She bit her tongue to keep from saying anything and took another bite of chicken. Who was she to judge, really? She sighed.

"Why the big sigh?"

"I was just thinking about my father. And Eric. Damn it, Dace, if he was involved in this drug smuggling stuff, I may swear off men for life. My experiences with them thus far have not been stellar."

He wiped his hands and face on a napkin and looked her in the eye for a long drawn out moment before he gathered up the remains of his meal and stuffed it in a paper bag. "Now that would be a damn shame. And such a waste. You have so much to offer a man. More than I could ever hope to have for myself. More than someone like me deserves, for sure." He gestured to the mess sitting in front of her on the table. "Are you done?"

"Yeah."

He shoved her trash into the bag as well, stood up and dumped everything in the garbage can, then came over to her, took her hands in his and pulled her to her feet.

She looked in his eyes and stepped closer. He really believed what he'd said. And it was so not true. "You've got that ass-backward, Detective. I've never wanted anyone the way I want you. Part of me says ignore it and another part says I might be missing out on the best thing that's ever happened to me. I don't want to be the woman I used to be anymore, but just seeing you makes me forget why I don't."

The blue flame in his eyes warmed her to the deepest, darkest parts of her. Parts she didn't know existed until that moment. He cupped her jaw in his hand and she tilted her head into it while he threaded his fingers in her hair. He lifted her face to take her mouth, holding it captive. Surely it wasn't years of abstinence that made his kiss feel so good? The desire to get closer, to melt into him, become part of him was more than a mere physical longing, unlike anything she'd experienced before. When his tongue touched hers, she whimpered. *Whimpered for Christ's sake.*

That was her last coherent thought as she pressed herself along his length and melted into him. Luxuriated in every inch of his hardness, and thought she'd died and gone to heaven when he pressed his hips into her, his hand on her bottom in a counter pressure that sent her reeling.

His tongue did things to her mouth that left her aching with the desire for more southern parts of him to do the same to more southern parts of her. Her brain quit functioning and didn't resurface until the need to feel skin on skin became too urgent to ignore, more urgent than the desire to maintain the status quo of having every inch of *her* molded to every inch of *him*.

She moved her hand to the hem of his shirt and slid

it underneath, letting out a moan at the mere feel of the skin of his abdomen. Her hand stayed where it was because she couldn't decide which direction she wanted it to travel. Instead she pressed her fingers into him and his stomach muscles clenched in instant response. Sparks zinged up her arm and ricocheted around inside her, sending out ripples of sensation from every spot they landed, leaving her trembling in reaction. How could she cope with all of her skin touching his, if just touching him with her hand did *this*? Would she completely fall apart? She was *already* falling apart, and wanted to stop before she lost complete control. At the same time, she wanted it to go on forever.

He ended the kiss to trail his mouth along her jaw, and she sucked in air she didn't realize she needed until that moment, then let out a gasp when he grabbed her hands and held them behind her back. Being trapped against him, pressed into him from shoulder to ankle had her head spinning and her heart pounding. She writhed against him in an effort to do what her hands no longer could, nearly overwhelmed by her desperate need to have her hands on him, stroking him, running her fingers through his hair, over his rough cheeks, along his hard muscles.

His cheek pressed into hers, and she rubbed against it. *Good Lord.* His scruff felt better than any other man's kiss ever had. She couldn't stifle a moan at the thought of that scruff touching other, more intimate parts of her. His breath in her ear as he spoke had her stilling instantly, dissolving into a quivering mass incapable of movement. God, she thought she might die from the feel of him.

"We have to stop. Before we make a big mess of

everything. You're not some one night stand or a weekend fling to me. And I sure as hell don't want to be that for you."

He let go of her hands and stepped away from her. The burning intensity of his gaze telling her it was as all-consuming for him as it was for her. They actually did have some kind of connection that went beyond the physical. Didn't they? It wasn't just her. Was it?

"I screwed things up once getting involved with a co-worker. The last thing I need right now is more of that shit. Nothing personal. If my life wasn't such a mess right now, we'd be in your bedroom, and I wouldn't give a damn if you were using me or not, until after the fact."

She took in a ragged breath and turned a shoulder toward him in an effort to clear her head. *She did not want to mess this up.* She squeezed her eyes shut, and a couple tears leaked out. Not what she was going for. She'd closed them to keep the tears *in*. She breathed slowly in then out through her nose in an effort to stop the shaking.

Was he right? Did her feelings go beyond the physical desire he aroused? Was that why they were so mind-blowingly intense? The thought of using him to satisfy a long dormant physical need was bitter and made her stomach turn. She *didn't* want to use him. She was a woman in a world dominated by men, but she was no longer that girl who lived by the motto, '*what's good for the gander is good for the goose.*'

She didn't need to be like that to feel equal to them. Not anymore. Not ever again. And *he* didn't want to treat *her* that way either. Another of the plethora of reasons he deserved her respect. Her voice cracked when she said, "Thank you." It took several attempts to swallow the lump in her throat before she could continue. "I wasn't using you."

His, "Good," came out like a sigh of relief.

It took a long time after he left before she wound down enough to sleep.

****

The following morning, while she quickly changed into her uniform and longed for another cup of coffee to counteract the effects of minimal sleep, she wondered how Dace had slept. After one look in the bathroom mirror, Sage reminded herself of the decision she'd made last night: quitting Caribbean Seas, finding a job on dry land and getting away from Dace was all part of her getting-on-with-her-life plan. He was a complication, mostly because she wasn't in a place to have a relationship right now.

Yes, she seemed to be moving toward that place, but not there yet. And yes, she was running away rather than facing her issues, just like he was, but she had bigger things than her psyche to take care of at the moment.

Her boss for instance. Why had she been summoned to Captain Southerby's quarters? Had something happened either on board or with the investigation in New Orleans while she and Dace were in Belize? If that was the case, surely he would have summoned one or both of them last night. Maybe something happened over night. She shook her head at the idea. After all, she wasn't really working on the investigation, merely giving Dace access to the information he needed. There was no need for the captain to update her. Had she messed up in her new job? Had they found someone to replace her at the end of this cruise?

"Stop it, Sage!" she said out loud. "You know paranoia's not a good thing." She came to a momentary halt when she entered the captain's quarters and saw Dace there. Maybe the meeting did have to do with drug smuggling and murder.

"Glad you could join us Dr. Brady," Southerby said. "Have a seat, please. This won't take long."

She didn't dare look at Dace as she made her way to the empty seat in front of the broad teak desk, finding it hard to believe such a short time had passed since the first time they sat like this. So much had happened in just a few days, it felt like weeks since she'd learned Eric had been murdered. She quickly sat in the empty chair, crossed her legs, and wrapped her hands tightly around her top knee, but stopped herself from kicking her foot back and forth. Since Captain Southerby didn't look happy, she feared maybe she was in trouble.

It had been a long time since she'd been taken to task. One episode with her father as the hospital director had been enough for her to vow it would never happen again. At least this time it wasn't going to be for inappropriate behavior with an intern. *Damn it.* Technically there had been improper behavior with a patient of hers... How had she managed to forget that detail? Maybe because of the investigation, and the ruse of them being involved, Dace didn't consider himself a patient?

Of its own accord, her gaze landed on Dace. It didn't help that the smoldering blue of his eyes was focused on her legs. Her heart picked up its pace. She turned her attention to his hands as he wiped them down his thighs like he was drying them off. Or was he wishing they were touching her legs in the same manner as his eyes? *Damn.* Of all the times to have her mind wander, a meeting with the captain was not it. And it certainly wasn't the time to realize, if she was getting sucked into doing inappropriate things with a patient, she may not be ready for life on dry land.

"Sir—"

The captain held up a hand in a silent order for her to keep quiet. "Since I have a few minutes, I wanted to touch base with you, get an update on the investigation, Detective, as well as ask you, Dr. Brady, if you have anything to report."

He paused, looking from one to the other, Sage resisted the urge to squirm in her seat like a six year old. She wasn't really in trouble, but this whole scenario made her guilty conscience take flight.

The captain made an irritated noise at their silence. "Mr. Langdon, any updates on your end?"

With the question, Sage glanced at Dace. Was he going to say anything about what Sean had done? He caught her glance and gave her a slight nod. The question must've been written all over her face. Or maybe they were just that in tune… *Not going there.*

"Actually, yes. If you hadn't summoned me, I would've gone looking for you. Has Sean Devlin's room been searched? Were any drugs found if it was? My boss has the pictures I took, and I need to know if we have any hard evidence."

The captain shook his head. "He was clean. Nothing on him and nothing in his room or belongings. The Chief of Security has orders to keep an eye on him, but to make sure no one else knows what's going on.

155

Do what you need to do, to find more evidence, Mr. Langdon. It's possible what Sean Devlin was doing yesterday has no relation to Dr. Roberts' death. Until we know exactly what he's doing, we're treating him as innocent until proven guilty. There's no solid proof it was a drug deal at that café, other than pictures of what looks suspiciously like drugs being transferred. Dr. Brady, I want you to keep an eye on Sean in a medical capacity. If he is involved in illegal activities, it's possible he's smuggling the drugs internally and that could cause other sorts of problems, as I'm sure you're aware."

Sage nodded. "I dealt with similar incidents in Chicago more times than I'd like to count. Should I say anything to Dr. Middleton, since he's Sean's doctor?"

"No!"

The captain and Dace spoke at the same time, then the captain continued, "Keep an eye on his file, and if he comes into the infirmary, try to be the one to care for him. *No one* in the medical department is to know about this. Until the New Orleans P.D. arrests someone, they're all under suspicion. After you discovered the prescription drugs being smuggled in the dispensary, I've subtly tightened the security on the infirmary so there's always a guard nearby. Since we're trying to keep this under wraps, I'd like to use a different strategy for the last few days of the cruise. This is where you come in Mr. Langdon. Your injury gives you good reason to be in the infirmary on a regular basis."

"We've been using that to our advantage," Dace said. "Dr. Brady and I are pretending a romantic interest in each other, letting people think we knew each other before I started working on the ship. It's why we spent the afternoon in Belize together."

The captain nodded his approval. "Use it as an excuse to drop by the infirmary on a regular basis as well. You need to do something to make your attachment more obvious. As captain, I'm not totally in the loop when it comes to gossip, but I have been keeping my ears open when I'm around the crew, and haven't heard anything that would help your investigation. Nor have I heard anything about you two having a...fling. I've made sure the Chief of Security knows about the drug smuggling, and had him station you, Mr. Langdon, in that part of the ship when you're on duty. Of course, he knows about Sean's suspicious activity in Belize."

Sage's shoulders and jaw muscles relaxed when there was no mention of a problem with her and Dace being involved. Maybe the temporary nature of being anyone's doctor on a cruise ship blurred the lines of acceptable behavior between a doctor and their patient. Still, it was a fine line. She chewed the inside of her lip. Who was she kidding? She forced herself to focus on the conversation.

Dace gave her a quick look before he spoke. "Hopefully we'll have useful information soon. For myself, I'd like to know the identity of the murderer before the end of this cruise, whether or not it's connected to the smuggling. Though, if we don't figure out who's doing the smuggling by the time we're back in N'awlins, the authorities may catch them transporting the drugs off the ship."

"Which is where you may prove to be invaluable Dr. Brady, since there's no reason for your presence in the dispensary to be questioned, you can keep an eye on that bottle and see if anyone is trying to transport it off the ship. Or at the very least, know that it's gone missing."

Sage's stomach burned at the captain's statement with both fear and anger. She knew she could handle herself when under attack, but a smuggler or a killer was a whole different level of violence. "Whatever I can do to help, Captain."

"I know that, Dr. Brady. It's why you've been asked to help. Now, it's Formal Night and you're both assigned to the reception, and dinner at the captain's table. Occasionally, I select a lower ranking officer to join us in order to give them experience dealing with passengers. I thought it would be a good opportunity for you to observe some of the officers, Detective. Dr. Brady won't be the only medical officer present. It's a little out of the ordinary, but I don't think it will raise any suspicion."

Chapter Eleven

The last thing Dace wanted to admit was that he'd really done a number on his arm yesterday in Belize, but he was done with being stupid. He lackadaisically watched the comings and goings in the dispensary's waiting room while waiting his turn to be seen. Since the captain wanted him to keep an eye on the infirmary, in the eyes of the Chief of Security, Dace was 'working'. Some of those waiting were the ship's crew, but the majority were passengers there to see Sage.

Truth be told, he wouldn't have minded seeing Dr. Middleton about his arm. It would give him the chance to observe him, see if he could learn anything that might prove whether he was real suspect, or merely one on paper. He'd suggested it to the receptionist when he saw how busy Sage was, but she said something about him being Dr. Brady's patient and it needed to stay that way. He considered coming back when she wasn't so swamped, but goosebumps on his skin, and the throb of his arm kept him in his seat.

Please God, don't let it be one of those funky staph infections you hear about on the news.

As the minutes ticked away, and everyone had their turn to see the doctor except him, he seriously considered she might be avoiding him. Not that it mattered really. If he wasn't in such a precarious medical situation, he'd be avoiding her. He'd enjoyed his share of attractive women, even became emotionally involved, but never had they been someone of Sage's caliber. Smokin' hot, highly intelligent and well-educated. He'd always considered someone like that out of his league.

He was hunched over in his seat, staring at his hands clasped between his legs, and barely concealed how startled he was when Celeste sat in the chair next to him. He most definitely wasn't up to par. "How are you doing, Mr. Langdon?"

"I've been better, *chère*, I'll admit."

"Dr. Brady will fix you up right. Sorry you've had to wait so long, but you can come back now. If it makes you feel any better, I think she was saving the best for last."

Dace chuckled. "Now that does make me feel better. Lead the way."

Once they were in the exam room, Celeste took his vitals, logged them on his chart, told him to remove his shirt, and left him alone. After about five minutes he gave in to the urge to lie back on the exam table and close his eyes. Sleep had been elusive the last few nights and exhaustion was getting the better of him. He closed his eyes and draped an arm across his forehead. If he hadn't felt chilled, he probably would've dozed off. As it was, his thoughts kept returning to Belize. The helplessness he'd felt when he saw Sage with a knife pointed at her. How slow he'd been to react. The desperation to give the thug what he wanted so he'd leave them alone. All reactions a policeman *shouldn't* be having. His gut churned from all of it.

Donato's death couldn't have messed his head up that badly. He certainly wasn't as emotionally involved with Sage as he had been with Donato. *No*. It was because he was sick. He wasn't functioning on all cylinders. Once his arm healed properly and this infection was out of his system, he'd be back to his old self. He refused to think about what he would do if that wasn't the case. He just needed to get well, that was all. With that, his stomach settled.

Sage taking his hand and squeezing it gently had his eyes flying open. How long had he been lying there? The sensations aroused by her hand made his stomach act up again. He wasn't sure if he wanted to punch something or kiss her senseless. Neither of which were a good idea. He settled for pulling his hand free and struggling to an upright position.

"You're not doing very well, Mr. Langdon."

"Not really, no," he growled.

"Your temp is up, though not a lot, which tells me the infection is getting the better of you. Does your arm feel any different than it did yesterday?" She left his side and went to the sink to scrub up. She turned to face him as she donned some gloves.

"The cut seems the same, I just feel worse overall. I opened it up again when I pinned that punk to the ground."

"Jesus, Dace! Why didn't you say something last night?" She shook her head. "Never mind. I know you well enough now, I don't need an answer. Although the captain has you keeping an eye on things here, I hope you'll take it easy."

Their eyes met, and though she didn't mask the sympathy she felt for what he was going through, there was something else there she was struggling to contain. He shouldn't be glad she wasn't as cool and aloof as she pretended, but he was. Not that he was going to let himself warm up to her, by any means. They were on the same page with that. He'd decided somewhere in the midst of trying to sleep last night that neither of them could afford to be a complication for the other. A quick roll in the hay wasn't going to cure what was between them. Only distance could do that. *And don't you dare forget it, Langdon.*

She gently peeled away the bandage and her brows pulled together as she looked at the wound. "Looks like the iodoform is doing its job, Dace, the edges of the wound look good, but you did open part of it up again and made it bleed. I really wish you could take time off to let this heal."

"Not happening. You know that already. But I will be careful. I promise."

"I'm going to hold you to it. Once I'm done with this I'm going to give you another shot of antibiotics. We need to get a handle on the infection."

****

"So, are you going to tell me about your afternoon in Belize with the hot new security guard?"

Sage was at her desk, trying to catch up on her files before she needed to get ready for dinner, when Celeste popped in. Normally she'd be happy for the interruption; this time it took all she had to suppress a scowl. She didn't want to talk about Dace, she didn't want to think about him, she didn't want to eat dinner at the same table as him. She wanted to get away from him before she did something stupid. And sleeping with him was only the tip of the stupid-iceberg.

She closed the laptop, leaned back in her chair and bit back a sigh. She gestured at the chair as an offer for her friend to sit.

Celeste plopped down, an expectant look on her face. "So? You gonna share the juicy details of your afternoon with him? It looks like things have moved out of the friend zone for you two. Am I right or am I right?"

Sage wanted to cringe, but she forced a small smile instead. She hated deceiving Celeste but reminded herself it was for a good cause. He definitely was hot. Maybe too hot for her to handle. Which was a new one. "How about this for a first date. I almost got robbed at knife point, but I took down the guy with my judo skills. Dace held him captive until the cops arrived. It was pretty sexy seeing him pin the guy to the ground with a knee in his back and hold him there with his arm jacked up behind him, just shy of breaking it. The reality, however, isn't quite so sexy."

She stifled the urge to laugh at the look of disappointment on Celeste's face. "Yeah, he didn't do that having wild sex with me, sorry. Besides, I don't do that anymore, remember? Relationship first, then sex."

She raised her brows, a skeptical look on her face. "So *nothing* happened?"

Sage shook her head. She didn't want to think about that kiss, much less talk about it. "I'm not saying I wasn't tempted but we both agreed to take things slow. The fact he's my patient right now being the least of the reasons. Been there, done that, not *ever* doing it again, by the way."

Celeste let out a resigned sigh. "I get that. And I don't want you to go there either."

"I know you don't. You're a good friend."

"You take your responsibilities seriously, Sage.

Even if you don't think so, I know so. You wouldn't be involved with this guy if it wasn't something serious."

If she only knew the real reason... Still, Sage smiled and some of the tension left her shoulders. It was ingrained since childhood to feel like everything she did was less than adequate, that she could've done better if she really tried.

"Yeah, there's something about Dace..."

"See? Important. Besides, I like that you're a doctor who cares a little more than she should sometimes. I understand the need for emotional distance, but you never take that too far. I've seen how you look at him sometimes. That you enjoy touching him a little more than you should."

"Oh, God," Sage groaned. "Have I done something inappropriate without realizing it?"

Celeste quickly shook her head. "No, no, not at all. Don't worry about that. It's because I know your story, I'm a little more tuned in, is all. And to be honest, I sometimes find it hard to believe your story, based on the Sage I've known for several years."

"This is why I love you, my friend. You always make me feel better about myself. I've told you how things were for me in Chicago and you like me anyway."

She gave her a teasing smile and a wink. After Celeste smiled back, she sobered. She really should be working, but she also felt the need to get another person's perspective on things. "It's just... I don't know, I genuinely like the guy, not just like looking at him. My feelings for him are—different than what I felt for my other boyfriends. If only the timing didn't suck."

"We've had our share of good times ogling men

both on and off the ship. I can tell it's not the same for y'all this time. It seems to me he's more than eye candy for you."

Sage swiped a hand down her face. "Maybe not, but frankly, whatever it is, I don't need the complication of it. I've got enough going on right now. The position of Chief Medical Officer is a lot to handle on top of Eric's death. And now, I'm not sure if I even want the job, to be honest."

"Lordy! Do you think Dace is part of the reason why?"

Yikes. This discussion was getting complicated. And even though Celeste wasn't a suspect, she didn't like putting one over on her friend. She looked down at her desk, closing her eyes for a moment to regroup. Maybe Dace was part of the reason she wanted to work on dry land again. If she was working in New Orleans, there was a better chance she'd run into him. If so, then she really needed to examine her motives.

"My ego really wants it but I'm not sure it's actually what *I* want. For the first time since I've worked for Caribbean Seas I feel like I've been wasting my time and skills."

Though uncomfortable that she'd shared so much with Celeste before she was positive it was the right decision, it felt good to talk about it at this moment. To hash it out somewhere besides inside her head.

"Wow…" Celeste pushed a blond curl off her forehead in her trademark gesture of frustration. "Actually, since Dr. Roberts' death, I've been thinking about moving on, getting more serious about my career. It's not being able to work with you that's had me hesitating more than anything."

Sage uncrossed her arms before leaning back in her chair. She laced her hands behind her head. "See? This is why we're such good friends. I'm not making any final decisions until I've had a chance to sort my feelings about Eric, but we definitely need to talk about this more. I'm glad you stopped in, Celeste. I'm feeling better already." She dropped her hands, squinted her eyes and her chair creaked as she leaned forward. Celeste was naturally pale, but even so she seemed to have less color in her face than normal. "You on the other hand, don't look so good. When's the last time you tested your blood sugar?"

"Hell, you're as bad as my mother. I may or may not have been drinking some last night… They were fine when I checked them a little while ago."

Sage winced. "I can't help it. It's the doctor in me. Glad they're okay, but diabetics shouldn't be drinking alcohol. You look awful."

Celeste wrinkled her nose. "Thanks for the compliment."

"That's what friends are for, right? I hate to push you out the door, but I'm way behind on stuff, and I have the reception and Formal Dinner with the captain tonight, so I can't catch up eating dinner at my desk."

"Enough said. I'll see you later."

The smile was still on her face long after Celeste left. Friends like her were hard to come by, and she was glad they'd had a chance to catch up a bit. It was just what she needed. Her smile slipped then vanished. Her day was a long way from being over.

Dinner with the captain and Dace was the least of it. It was more than a day since she'd been inside the dispensary for reasons other than filling a prescription.

Though she was a bit worried about what she might learn, it was something that would bug her until she knew. Had anything happened with that bottle while she was gone? With the hospital empty of patients and medical staff on-call for the rest of the day, this was a perfect opportunity to look at the contents of the bottle of smuggled hydrocodone and see if anyone had used it. She pushed her chair back from the desk and headed to the dispensary.

She had a hard time locating the bottle in the cupboard and she made damn sure everything was put back exactly as it had been before she high-tailed it out of there. As she left the infirmary, heading for Dace's cabin, she couldn't shake the returning feeling that she was being watched. Again while she was at work. And her instincts had been spot on in Belize…

Damn! This situation was making her paranoid, and she wished she just knew who the bad guy was so she didn't expect danger at every turn. Was the smuggler watching her every time she was at work? Every time she accessed the dispensary? It was ridiculous to think that. He, or she, couldn't be there 24/7, and certainly couldn't be working the exact same hours as her. She knew that for a fact since she made up the schedule. She picked up her pace anyway and pounded on his door as soon as she reached it. He needed to know what she'd discovered before they went to dinner. The butterflies in her stomach had nothing to do with seeing him again. Really. *They didn't.* As she waited for him to answer, she checked her watch. Almost two hours before dinner. She let out a breath in relief. They had some time yet. She banged on the door again.

"Dace! Are you in there?"

She hadn't seen him in the infirmary or in the general vicinity, so she'd assumed he was off duty. Had something come up? Was he okay? Had she been so distracted by his presence she'd missed how sick he really was today? She smothered a curse and pounded on the door a couple more times muttering,

"Please be here, damn it. I need you."

He opened the door just in time to hear the last bit. Not a good thing. He gave her a slow smile, pulled her into his cabin, and slammed the door. "Hell, woman, you really shouldn't say things like that. Makes me wanna show you how much I need you."

He braced his hands on the door on either side of her head. His proximity, the fire in his gaze as it roamed her face, much less the fact he wasn't wearing a shirt, had her forgetting why she was really there, and wishing she was there for more carnal reasons. Oddly, at the same time, being with him was a comfort. Her fear and panic subsided.

She looked into the fiery blue of his eyes and placed her hands on his cheeks, moving them up and down ever so slightly. She loved the feel of his scruff. The friction of his stubble sent sparks from her hands to every nerve ending in her body, and the sensation was becoming addictive. Why weren't they supposed to be doing this? For the life of her she couldn't remember. *Damn...* She'd hardly done anything and she could feel those sensations from the top of her head to the tips of her toes.

"Never in my life has such a bad idea seemed like such a good one. You're going to drive me mad, woman, by the time I solve this case."

He threaded his fingers through her hair and focused his attention on her mouth, making her lips ache to feel his. She seriously doubted she would drive him as mad as he was driving her, however, he was right about one thing. This was a bad idea. She needed to tell him something important. She needed him to back off so she could *think*.

"Dace—"

He caressed her cheekbones with his thumbs, and the words she planned to say vanished. She stifled a moan and bit her lip. This was probably the worst time ever to realize the feelings she had for Dace went way beyond anything she'd felt before with any man. One look into his eyes, his slightest touch on her face, and she felt like she was home. When she was with him she didn't ever want to be anywhere else.

"What brings you to my room in such a panic, Sage, that had you banging on my door, rousing me from some much needed sleep? Not that it isn't nice to know you're in need of me for once. Is it because you're pretending to be my girlfriend?" He gave her a lopsided smile and closed the small amount of distance between them, pressing her back against the door. "And now you're here, I've discovered how urgently I need you."

She closed her eyes, suddenly very well aware of what his needs were when he pressed himself into her. Before she could stop herself, she rubbed against him in an invitation for more. She shook her head. Both as an attempt to clear it and to tell him 'no'. She *needed* to tell him no. She really did. She wasn't going to let excessive stress dictate her actions anymore. Why did such a wonderful man have to come into her life at such a horrible time?

"Dace please… This is hard enough as it is."

"Mmmm…" He buried his face in her neck and ground his hips into her. "Don't I know it?" he growled. "I can't imagine being any harder than I am right now."

Sage moaned, the blood thundering in her ears, his hot breath on her neck, the roughness of his cheek scraping against her sensitive skin sending a shower of sparks down her body and lighting a fire everywhere his length touched hers. How was she supposed to find the strength to stop this madness? Hopping into bed with the most sexy, gorgeous, wonderful man she'd ever run across was not how she wanted to cope with all that was going on aboard the ship.

What kind of cruel joke was it that she had to meet him *now?* Was her desire to be with him merely because she was dealing with so much, and hadn't been with a man in so long? Were those things amplifying her feelings? Or was what she felt for Dace physically and emotionally truly much deeper? The angst of trying to answer those questions alone was enough to make her say 'to hell with it,' and give in to what her body, her heart, was clamoring for.

Suddenly Dace stiffened, let go of her and backed away, the decision taken out of her hands."Damn, Sage, what is it with you that makes it nearly impossible for me to think straight? I was sleeping when you banged on the door, and still out of it when I opened it. It didn't help to have you saying you need me, either."

He turned around and walked over to his bed, sinking down onto it as he motioned for her to take the single chair the room had to offer. His cabin was like a miniature version of a hotel room, and she cursed the cramped quarters. She really wanted a big chunk of space between them so she could get her head straight, not have the only place they could go, be his bedroom. Seeing him sitting on the bed, the covers a mess from his having been in it, being close enough to feel his heat, to get a whiff of his male scent. It was nearly impossible to think about anything but pushing him down on the bed and finishing what they'd started at the door. It made her ache all over and she couldn't remember why she was there.

He combed his fingers through his hair in an attempt to combat bedhead, then scrubbed his hands down his face. "So, what's happened to put you in such a panic?"

That's right. She'd been really freaked out when she got here. For good reason. Suddenly her physical need for Dace dissipated.

"I checked the bottle of ibuprofen to see if anyone messed with it while we were gone. First of all, it had been moved, so it took me a while to find it. That was enough to worry me. When I counted the pills, there was only one missing. It was the real ibuprofen we put in there."

The words he said weren't pretty. Colorful, but not pretty. Her sentiments exactly.

"Yeah. Now you know why I was so freaked out."

He didn't say anything, just let out a frustrated sigh and scooted along the bed to sit right across from her. "Whoever is doing this just upped the ante. I don't want you going near that bottle again. No one saw you messing with it, did they?"

"Jesus, Dace, I'm not an idiot. The bottle was hard to find. At first I thought it was gone. But with that pill

Robyn Rychards

missing, I'm worried they're sending me a message. That they know I know."

"They might be. Or they may have removed the pill because they don't want to get in trouble with whomever they're planning on selling the drugs to. Or…"

"Or what?"

His mouth quirked for a moment, then he shrugged. "The bottle being hidden and the missing pill doesn't mean Dr. Roberts isn't our guy. It could mean someone else realized the pills weren't ibuprofen and doesn't want anyone handing them out by mistake. They could've taken the ibuprofen we put in there and put it back in the right bottle merely because it wasn't supposed to be there. If that's the case, they will either report it to the captain or to you. I'll get in touch with Captain Southerby to see if anyone's done that since we spoke to him earlier. That having been said, we'll assume the worst, hope for the best, and go with the assumption the culprit *is* sending a message. Which means we need to send one back. The smuggler may not know that it's you in particular who's figured out their game, but you're definitely going to be on their list of suspects because you have access to the dispensary." He paused and narrowed his eyes at her before letting out a gusty sigh. 'We're going to have to make it very clear you're not an easy target."

"I'm rarely by myself, so I don't think that's really a problem and I can be extra vigilant about it. I'm the boss. I can make sure there's always someone around."

He looked at her in silence for long drawn out seconds before he looked away. She didn't like the look on his face when he returned his attention to her, and

172

when he stood up and went to lean against the door, her heart rate quickened.

"We're going to have to take things to the next level." He paused and chewed his bottom lip for a moment.

"What exactly do you mean by next level?"

His gaze roamed her face before he studied his feet.

"If you don't say something soon, I might have to hit you. You're freaking me out."

He looked back up at her, an odd expression on his face. "You realize any one of those times you're not alone, when another colleague is working with you, *that* could be the person we're looking for. It's time we made it more obvious you and I are together. In a serious way. Some PDA in front of the crew, and my moving into your cabin is probably the most effective way to do that. It makes you less of an easy target. With a security guard for a boyfriend, they may think twice about trying something."

"Not happening. Seriously stupid idea for a lot of reasons."

"Doesn't matter. I couldn't live with myself if something happened to you."

Was that terror that flashed through his eyes? Was he as worried about her has he had been about Donato? She stifled the happiness the thought evoked.

"Any other options? Not that I don't like having you around. And not that I think I can't take care of myself. But I'm not stupid either. I've been around enough gang members and drug dealers working in Chicago to know better."

It was the look on his face that made her cave. She

stifled a groan. *Great. Two days of playing hot and heavy with Officer Dark and Dangerous.*

"Not that I can think of. Let me know if you come up with anything. In the meantime, making it obvious we're in a serious relationship at the crew member's bar after dinner tonight might be in order."

Chapter Twelve

Dace pushed away from the door and hunted up his duffel bag so he could pack up his stuff. Until someone was arrested, he'd either be with Sage or back to doing his regular job on dry land. He prayed it was the latter as soon as the boat docked in New Orleans.

He pulled out his phone and called Rocque while he collected up his few personal items and shoved them in his bag.

"Dace. What can I do you for?"

"Just hoping for some new info on your end. Anything on Sean Devlin?"

"Can't help you much there. The guy's clean. I let DEA know the name of the café, and what you saw there, but they didn't tell me much. Since you didn't find anything in his cabin, and there's no real connection with Dr. Roberts, you might want to ignore him. Or at least as far as the deal you saw going down in Belize. Not our jurisdiction, not our problem. DEA can deal with it. John Middleton, on the other hand…"

Dace went on full alert. "Did you find something?"

"His prints were at the crime scene, however, he was Dr. Roberts' colleague, so it's purely circumstantial, as it wouldn't be unreasonable for Middleton to make a social call on him."

"Are you trying to make me crazy, Cap? Tell me you have more—something to have you thinking I need to snoop around."

"It's just the little things starting to add up. There's been some significant deposits into Middleton's bank account with no way to account for their source. However, there's also some circumstantial evidence that a local drug dealer could be our killer. Or, more specifically, paid for a hit on Roberts. Drug dealers don't kill to make it look like a heart attack. They hire someone to do that for them."

His stomach sank as he dropped his toothbrush and toothpaste into his bag. He pinched the bridge of his nose. Sage had trusted Roberts. Cared about him. She wouldn't like to know he was the one smuggling prescription drugs. "What else do you got that points to Roberts?"

"Cash deposits into his bank account as well. We have a witness who picked a drug dealer out of photographs which place him in the vicinity of Roberts' home on more than one occasion. However, said drug dealer has been picked up for selling prescription drugs in Roberts' neighborhood, and it could be selling drugs was the only reason he was there. It's a mess we're still trying to untangle. Just keep an eye on Middleton, and see if you can get us anything more concrete. We still have some leads we're following here. I'll let you know if anything pans out with those."

"I'll be back on dry land in two days. Are you gonna let me stay there?"

"Ha Ha. I need some one-on-one with you to decide that, officer. Call me tomorrow to check in."

Dace bit back a sigh of frustration, not wanting to ruin his chances for getting back to his real job. "Will do."

After ending the call, he shoved the phone into his pocket. As he pulled his supply of uniforms out of the closet and threw them on the bed, he hoped the evening at the captain's table would be the distraction he needed to keep from obsessing about Sage being held at knife point. He'd tried like hell to convince himself she was no more important to him than any other citizen but the chills up his spine and a twisting gut told him otherwise. The attempted mugging haunted him when he slept. Every time he closed his eyes and drifted off, the night Donato was killed replayed in his head. Then, instead of Donato lying there bleeding to death, it morphed into Sage, the mugger poised over her with a bloody knife.

When he forced himself to not think about Sage in danger, his mind switched to thoughts more dangerous to him on a personal level. How magnificent she'd looked, giving that thug what-for. The sparkle in her eyes, the defiant jut of her chin. She wasn't one to back down. Certainly not to him. Her beautiful face and luscious curves were deceptive. She was no pretty girl wanting to be pampered.

She'd proved herself worthy and made sure everyone knew her looks had nothing to do with her achievements. How she handled him the first day he laid eyes on her proved that, much less when she stood up to the mugger. That had to be why he was so obsessed with her. No doubt it would wear off. The sooner the better.

****

His seat assignment at the Captain's table made him wonder if Southerby knew more than he'd let on in their meeting. The round table sat ten people, big enough so that conversation was limited to the people on either side of him. Dr. Middleton was seated on his left; Sage, however, was across from him, which meant he wouldn't be talking with her until they went to the bar later. It wasn't long, though, before he realized he enjoyed watching her throughout the meal. More than was good for him probably. He had a sinking feeling he could look at her for the rest of his life and never tire of it.

The Captain's Formal Dinner was a new experience for more than the fact this was his first cruise. He'd never attended anything so posh, and was glad he had a uniform to wear, instead of a tuxedo, like the male passengers. The reception before the meal was something else to add to his list of firsts and was very glad to have his experience as a cop to fall back on. Being sociable, knowing how to deal with people was a handy skill to have. He also used the opportunity to observe fellow officers, John Middleton included. One never knows what another person might give away over canapes or champagne cocktails.

Once everyone was seated and the meal orders were taken, he forced himself to stop thinking about Sage and how miserable this blasted infection made him feel, and focus on doing his job. Questioning Dr. Middleton without him realizing he was being interrogated was a snap under usual circumstances. He prayed he was up to the task but a lack of sleep and a compromised immune system were a bad combination. His stomach growled. Well, at least the infection wasn't interfering with his appetite. The smell of fresh baked bread wafting around him didn't help either. He could probably ask someone to pass him the bread basket, but as he wasn't operating at the top of his game, he didn't want to miss an opportunity because he was too busy scarfing down bread.

Fortunately for everyone, the doctor himself got the ball rolling. "I'm John Middleton, the staff's doctor. Are you new to the ship or new to Caribbean Seas?"

"Dace Langdon. New hire actually, and this is my first trip. How about you?"

"I've been working for the line for almost nine years now."

"You must really like it, then."

Dace smiled and turned slightly toward him in his seat, hoping he came across as a new employee eager to know more about his employer, but it also gave him a better view of the man's demeanor and body language. Middleton gave a big smile but his fingers tightened around his water glass. Because Dace sat right next to him, he saw the slight stiffening in his body.

"It pays well and I've always liked traveling. In fact, I met my wife while working on a cruise. She was the Cruise Director. We had a lot of fun working together."

He relaxed as he started talking about his wife, and Dace sensed his love for her. He nodded, settling into the role of eager new employee. "I liked the idea of traveling to new places and getting paid to do it. One day I was surfing the net to see what I needed in order to work for a cruise line. When I discovered my old friend Sage Brady was working for one, I was sold. I think it's great couples can work together on Caribbean Seas." He looked across the table at Sage, pretty sure the smitten look on his face was genuine. Certainly not part of the plan when he started this ruse, but definitely helpful in the moment. "The job's not quite as glamorous as I thought, but I like it. Are you working with your wife on this particular cruise?"

The doctor frowned and shook his head before sipping from his glass of water. Dace mimicked the move in an effort to put him at ease. His question had touched a nerve and he wanted to know why. As finding out might prove tricky, he remained silent to see if the doctor would elaborate. In general, guys didn't ask other guys such personal questions. Women asked stuff like that. As well as cops who needed information. A rookie mistake he wasn't going to make.

"She quit when she got pregnant with our daughter four years ago and was determined to be a stay-at-home mom. I'm the sole breadwinner now. And there are times when I miss that extra paycheck. So, you look pretty smitten with Sage. Are you and she together?"

For effect, Dace looked at Sage again, smiling with what he hoped was an intimate smile, and prayed it covered up how disturbed he was by Middleton saying he looked smitten. "We are. Makes me wish I'd gotten to know her better back when we lived in Chicago. All those wasted years."

"I hope it works out for you two. I don't know her well, but the staff all seem to like her."

Without giving Dace a chance to comment, Middleton turned his attention to the woman on his other side. That move reminded Dace he had a job to do too, as far as the passengers were concerned. Still, he managed to enjoy watching Sage do the same thing for a few seconds before he engaged the man seated next to him in small talk.

They'd settled into their dinner and Dace was

almost through eating his steak when he started to wonder if he should try to strike up a conversation with the doctor again. He'd hoped Middleton would approach him, but after their initial conversation, he hadn't. Dace didn't want to lose the opportunity to learn something, but he didn't want to mess things up either. There was a reason he was a police detective and not an undercover cop, and this scenario pretty much summed it up. He didn't like pretending to be something he wasn't, and he didn't like trying to finagle information out of someone. Direct interrogation was more his style. As he popped a bite of steak in his mouth, he lifted his eyes to look at Sage, as though looking at her could somehow solve his dilemma. Which was rather stupid, since merely watching her as she was engaged in an animated conversation with a passenger was enough to make him forget everything.

What would he do when this job was over and they went their separate ways? How had he gotten through each day before he met her? Ever since she walked into the captain's quarters—*good God. was that only three days ago?*—his world revolved around the next time he was going to see her. What would happen to him when being with her wasn't part of his daily schedule?

He looked down at his plate and had a hard time swallowing the food in his mouth. Suddenly the juicy, melt-in-your-mouth piece of rib eye lost its appeal. His knife and fork clattered on his plate, and he grabbed his glass of water, wishing it was something stronger. Had his throat ever been this dry? Had he ever wanted anyone as much as he wanted Sage? In his bed? In his *life?* He could feel the sweat break out on his forehead at the thought.

Middleton couldn't have picked a better time to engage him in conversation. The distraction from his thoughts was a relief. "So how do you like working on a cruise ship so far?"

"It's early yet, but I don't think I'll have a problem sticking with it to fulfill my contract. How about you, after all these years? Are you planning on making it a life-time career?"

"It's a hard job when you have to leave your family for such a long period of time. Can't complain about steady work, though, when you have a lot of responsibilities."

"Responsibilities I'm certainly not ready to tackle yet. I admire you for sticking with it for so long. Caribbean Seas must be a good employer."

"I'm sure you don't have the kind of bills I have. I started off in debt with school loans. Now a family on top of it. I envy guys like you your freedom."

Dace looked down at his plate, concentrating on cutting another piece of steak. The doctor's resentment was unmistakable. *Envy me enough to commit murder, I wonder?*

"Tuition is definitely the downside of a higher education. Too bad not everyone takes their responsibilities as seriously as you."

"Yeah, well, loans they do wear you out. I recommend starting a family when you're financially able to take care of them properly."

"Advice I will definitely keep in mind." He chewed slowly as he looked over at Sage. Middleton didn't hide the bitterness that laced his tone. Is that what happened after a man had been married a while and started a family? Did a family start to feel like an anchor tying you down?

His gaze wandered around the giant dining room. All the elegantly dressed passengers enjoying the opportunity to get away from it all by living in a fantasy of luxury for a few days. Expensive food, tables covered with white linen, waiters and waitresses dressed in black, catering to their every need. When a delectable dessert was set in front of him, he let himself get sucked into the atmosphere, enjoying the moment, and he realized Rocque hadn't been punishing him, he'd done him a service. This escape from New Orleans was exactly what he needed.

When the entire wait staff gathered on the long, curved staircase that led down to the dining room and sang *That's Amore,* he took the time to watch Sage enjoy the performance.

As he was escorting her from the dining room, his heart jumped into his throat, then sank to his toes. The woman a few steps away was the last thing he needed right now. Their route to Sage's quarters suddenly needed to be one which kept them out of sight. Had Tina spotted him? He picked up his pace, but only a little, so Sage wouldn't guess they had a new problem. A quick exit to the deck before the woman who could complicate everything, much less blow his cover, spotted him.

"You know, I haven't been on deck to enjoy the view yet, and I'm sure it's an amazing one at night. Let's do that since we're so close, before we head back to the cabin to change out of our uniforms."

He didn't give her a chance to respond, just ushered her out the nearest exit and onto the deck. There were a few people milling about, but not near as many as were inside, and he spotted a deserted seating area.

"Wanna cuddle on the couch, or stand at the railing for the full effect?"

"The railing is fine. I don't think we need to play the happy couple out here. It's too dark and deserted. Our timing is perfect, though. The moon is just rising, something I haven't enjoyed very often over the past three years." She slanted him a narrowed look. "I'm not buying your reason for coming out here."

Why had he thought, even for a moment, he could fool her? He grabbed her hand and led her over to the railing. She was right, their timing was perfect. The moon was suspended over the ocean, its light reflecting off the water like a pathway of white, multitudes of stars dusting the sky. His breath caught at the beauty of a sight he'd never experienced, and he was glad for the chance to. More than that, he was experiencing it with a beautiful woman he cared about. Cared about more than was good for him probably.

"I saw an ex-girlfriend as we were leaving the dining room; she was headed my way. I don't think she saw me, but I certainly don't need her to blow my cover. I can't believe I haven't run into her before tonight."

"Not good," Sage murmured. "How long has she been your ex? Do you think she'll buy your career change?"

He grabbed the railing and looked down at his feet as he pondered the question, then looked back at the moon as though it might provide an answer. "I don't know if she'll buy it. We'd only been going out a couple months and didn't know each other real well. I broke up with her after Donato was killed. She was pretty pissed about it, but she was getting clingy and I didn't want to deal with her crap on top of everything else going on. She may still be pissed for all I know. I didn't notice a male companion with her. This cruise could be her attempt to get over me." He shook his head at himself. "That's a bit egotistical, I guess, but this is exactly why I don't do undercover for more than a day. I hate the deception. It messes with my head."

Sage turned to face him, leaning her hip on the railing, but after a glance he kept his eyes fixed on the horizon. They were traveling south, the moon was rising in the east, giving the appearance it was making the journey with them. The laughter from a group of people on the deck below drifted up to them and he envied them for a moment. To be out here savoring this view as part of a fabulous vacation, rather than hiding from an ex.

"So we need a story just in case we meet up with her, to make the time-line work."

"Yeah." Resigned, he blew out his breath. "And the one that works best is that I'm a two-timing jerk who dumped her after I decided I liked you better. Liked you enough to switch jobs to spend more time with you. The thing is, she knows exactly how much I love my job. I made it clear to her from day one that no woman took priority over my job, so she had to be content with second place."

Her extended silence after his statement had him squirming in his skin. Saying it out loud, to her especially, made him sound like a real asshole. Until that moment, he'd always felt he was doing his girlfriend a favor, letting her know from the get-go where she stood. No unrealistic expectations meant no issues down the line.

"Well, aren't you the real gentleman? You realize, some women would just take it as a challenge?"

He couldn't argue that one. "I think Tina Flannery might be one of them. Which means, painting me as a two-timing jerk is a good way to go. Also, finding out where her cabin is and avoiding that part of the ship is a good idea. I've made it more than halfway through the cruise before seeing her, here's hoping I can avoid her for two more days."

"Surely something can go right?"

He laughed. "Exactly. Let's take the outside stairs to the main deck. It's a lot easier to avoid people under cover of darkness."

It also helped that as a security guard, he knew the details of the ship's layout and all its entrances and exits. Many of which were crew access only. Sadly, right now they were in a public area of the ship, and until they reached the crew's quarters, running into Tina again was a possibility.

Damn it. When were things going to start going his way? Apparently not anytime soon because the minute he and Sage walked back into the ship proper, there she was walking toward them. The only thing working in his favor was that it appeared she hadn't spotted him yet. Before Tina had a chance to recognize him, he did the only thing he could think of. Something crew members shouldn't be doing in the public areas of the ship. He backed Sage up against the wall, plastered himself against her, hands braced on either side of her head, and kissed her like he couldn't get enough. Like he was so desperate for her he couldn't wait until they were in private. Exactly the way he'd been dying to since she walked into the captain's quarters on day one.

He rubbed his body the length of hers, moved his hips insinuatingly against her and plunged his tongue into her mouth. And, God help him, she gave as good as she got. No stiffening at the unexpectedness of it, no attempt to push him away, not one second taken to adjust to what was happening. In unison they went up in flames and neither of them gave a damn that it was in public, that it was taboo as members of the crew, or that it was the last thing they should be doing for their own sanity.

He should've been taking note of how long the kiss needed to last. Using his other senses to discern when the danger of being recognized was over, but he had no clue about any of that. The blood was rushing in his ears and heading south so quickly he couldn't hear anything else. His senses were tingling with the feel of her body so close to his, he was unaware of anything but her. How she felt, how she smelled, how she tasted. It was the closest thing to heaven he'd ever experienced and it consumed him. Devoured him. Enchained him.

Oh dear God, and when she writhed against him, running her leg up the side of his and resting her thigh on his hip, he thought he'd explode right then and there. He cursed the pencil thin skirt of her uniform which kept her from wrapping her legs around him and giving them both a modicum of relief, and ran a hand up her thigh, under the damn thing. Maybe if he hitched it high enough, she could wrap her legs around him…

The sudden twinge in his arm from the effort was enough to bring a moment of sanity, a sense of where he was, and the reality of what he was about to do.

He tore his mouth from hers and removed her leg from his hip instead, letting it fall back to the ground. He swore violently at himself, but not loud enough for anyone other than Sage to hear, and stepped back from her a pace to look both ways down the hall. Tina was long gone and another couple was walking away from them. Beating a hasty retreat from their R-rated display, most likely.

"I'm sorry, Sage. I didn't mean to climb all over you in public. My brain turns off when I get too close to you. I saw Tina and needed to do something before she recognized me. I didn't expect things to get out of control so quickly." He raked his fingers through his hair. "God I hope we're not called in by Southerby for another meeting. The kind of meeting neither of us want."

He gritted his teeth because, still, he was unable to look at anything but Sage. Her flushed cheeks, her bright red lips, the fire in her eyes were enough to draw him back into another kiss that would get them in serious trouble.

"Old habits die hard, I guess. It wouldn't be the first time I got taken to task for inappropriate PDA. I'm bad news, Dace. Best you realize that now, before I do something to really ruin you."

"Don't demean yourself. I'm a big boy and take responsibility for my own actions. It's bad enough I lost control. You've done nothing to warrant the crude, selfishness of being screwed against the wall in a hallway, no matter where that hallway happens to be. I'll work harder to make sure I handle things better if the situation arises again."

****

After an hour at the crew's bar, he was done. As wonderful as it was being in such close proximity to the beautiful doctor, sitting cuddled up in a booth with her, making small talk, playing nice with the crew members who stopped by their table to chat with Sage and meet him, he was beyond exhausted. He broke out in a cold sweat just thinking about how inappropriately he'd behaved, how little control he'd had over himself for the first time in his life.

Though Sage merely being herself was a big factor in that loss of control, he blamed his injury, and exhaustion. It wasn't like he hadn't kissed her before. But, *damn,* the way she'd responded sent him into a tailspin he almost didn't pull out of.

Sage having a boyfriend drew an inordinate amount of attention from the crew, and though it was what he wanted, it sounded better in theory than in practice. Though she'd told him she didn't get involved with anyone she worked with, he was surprised to learn it was the first time she'd been seen with a member of the opposite sex. He shouldn't be happy about that. She wasn't *really* his girlfriend for God's sake. His head kept telling him he wasn't interested in long term relationships, but he was having a hard time standing firm on that resolve. The more he was around her, the better a serious relationship sounded. Something more than the initial enjoy-each-other's-company thing he'd wanted to pursue at the start of the cruise.

His arm tightened, and he pulled her closer. His hand caressed her waist and moved to splay across her belly as he nuzzled her neck. He loved the way her breath caught in her throat when he did it.

This can't go anywhere, Langdon. Their bodies,

however, had a different agenda, and were ignoring their minds. It did make him wonder for a moment if this was another time he was better off listening to his gut.

"You're not taking advantage, are you Detective?"

"Of course I am, *chère*. Any hot blooded male will cop a feel with his girlfriend whenever the opportunity arises. And don't call me detective. Someone might overhear."

"Thanks for the heads up. Makes me feel special. Just don't try anything when we're alone. I have ways of hurting you, you've never dreamed of. I know a lot about the human body. That kiss in the hallway is not something I want repeated."

"Are you *trying* to turn me on?"

He took her chin and turned her head to look in her eyes. He noticed flecks of yellow in them for the first time, warming them, sucking him into their heat. They were in public. The crew needed to know they were a couple. He lowered his head and took her bottom lip between his teeth, lightly tugged on it and ran his tongue across it before plunging it into her mouth.

His breath was labored. He was shaking all the way to his core. *Jesus. Over a kiss? Not again.* He needed to stop this before things went above and beyond the call of duty. Still, it didn't stop the words tumbling out of his mouth. Gut instinct again?

"Time to go to your cabin, *chère*. Let's play doctor in private."

"Works for me."

The huskiness of her tone, the catch in her voice. He'd regained control of himself since that kiss in the hall, though his hard-on hadn't gone away, and he was determined not to do anything inappropriate again. Injury or not, certainly he could keep it together for two days. Then he could decide if pursuing Dr. Brady was a good idea or not. A new thought came to him. It was like a bucket of cold water over his head.

What if she was using him for stress relief?

****

Dace stood behind her, his hands caressing her hips as she unlocked the door to her cabin. Though she knew he was doing it for show, it took everything she could muster to unlock the door without her hands shaking, giving away how much his touch, his nearness, affected her. She forced herself to focus on *why* she wasn't going to let this chemistry they had get the better of her. Shoving the key in the lock with more force than necessary she twisted it and pushed the door open. *Damn... Why was it again?*

Once inside, she scooted out of his hold and went to the sitting area, leaving him to close the door. Feeling restless, she forced herself to sit in a chair and grabbed her laptop off the coffee table. Had she really tried to wrap her legs around him in public? Offering herself up to him with no thought to where they were or what might happen? What happened to years of discipline, of trying to change her ways? Did she need to accept the fact *that* Sage was the real her? That she was a leopard who couldn't change its spots? She put a hand to her stomach in an instinctive desire to cool the flames eating away at it. Maybe the best thing for her was to accept who she was and get on with her life.

No. She could do this. She wasn't going to use a man merely to feel good, and she certainly wasn't going to do it with a man like Dace, who deserved a much better woman than that.

She opened her laptop and looked over it at him as he hovered in the entrance of the room. Her brows drew together as she noted his paleness, and the dark shadows under his eyes. The man was not well. She set the laptop back on the table.

"You're seriously in need of a good night's rest, Dace. I want you to sleep in my bed. I'll be perfectly comfortable on the couch. What time is your shift tomorrow?"

"Noon to midnight. And the same the next day."

"I'm not happy with how slowly you're recovering. You need rest to heal and get well. Do you want me to get you something to help you sleep? It should be completely worn off by the time you go on duty."

He rubbed both hands down his face. "I don't think so. I'm supposed to be your personal security guard for the night, remember? Just need another dose of ibuprofen and I should be good." He pulled the bottle of pills out of his pocket and took one out.

"You need something to wash that down? There's bottled water in the mini fridge."

"Thanks. Do I need to stop by the infirmary tomorrow?"

He walked over and pulled one out, downing the pill, and the entire contents of the bottle of water in one go. The world tilted on its axis for a moment at the picture he made, and she didn't comprehend his question. It had to be the stress. And the fatigue. That had to be why the past suddenly reared its ugly head.

That awful night when she made the mistake of going to the ER dispensary to do inventory flashed before her eyes in all its technicolor glory. The sight of her father popping a pill and downing a bottle of water the same way Dace just did. The bottle of amphetamines he hadn't been prescribed sitting on the counter before he slipped them into his pocket... If only she'd waited until later. But things had been so slow and she was *bored.*

Not that he wouldn't have been caught at some point. Just that *she* wouldn't have been involved in the whole mess. And then he'd had the gall—the sheer, unmitigated gall—to take her to task for fooling around with someone she supervised because she'd called him on his 'habit'.

The unexpected memory was the reality check she needed. After everything that went down with her father, she promised herself she wasn't going care about anyone so much ever again, because in the end they let you down. She *would not* let these unexpected feelings she had for Dace get to that point. And she strongly suspected he was the one man it could happen with.

Relationships were complicated and here she was, contemplating having one with Dace because she was so attracted to him. Maybe she *could* use some therapy. She couldn't make heads or tails of what she wanted, and what was best for her, on her own. She sighed. The middle of a murder investigation certainly wasn't the time to be psychoanalyzing herself.

"Sage? Are you okay?"

She shook her head to dislodge the picture dancing before her eyes, then nodded when she realized he might think she meant 'no'. "Yes. Come by around eleven-thirty, before you start your shift. I'll be done seeing patients by then, so you don't need to worry about scheduling an appointment or anything."

"Sounds good. You're sure about the bed?"

"Absolutely."

"Thanks. Greatly appreciated."

His hot gaze roved over her and she held her breath, sure he was going to say—or do—something to weaken her resolve. Just thinking about him in her bed had her heart beating faster, her breath catching in her throat, butterflies batting around in her stomach like he was her first crush.

It was anti-climactic when he said nothing and turned around. Still, it didn't stop her admiring the view as he headed down the short hall to the bedroom. Then she remembered something she'd been meaning to tell him, but hadn't had the chance. "Oh, Dace?"

He paused, bracing his hands on the door frame as he looked over his shoulder at her. It was an image that didn't lend itself to her having an good night's sleep, but one she couldn't help but appreciate. "Yes?" He raised a brow with the question and her breath caught in her throat. Definitely going to keep her awake for a while. *Stop. It.*

"Thanks for staying here."

Not what she'd wanted to come out of her mouth. She took a deep breath. She'd done a lot of thinking about the drug smuggling/murder mystery and reached a conclusion she found hard to voice. Maybe because it made it more real. "I've been doing a lot of thinking about our suspects, as well as everyone on the staff. If I had to pick someone for this, it would be Eric."

Dace dropped his hands, crossed his arms, and leaned against the doorjamb to face her. "Interesting. What makes you say that?"

"Getting past my feelings and looking at it logically, it's the best explanation for everything. I think my perspective has been skewed because I wanted it to *not* be him so badly. As for Sean... And this has nothing to do with emotion either, but I can't see him killing anyone. I don't think he's involved in anything more than trying to pick up some recreational drugs for him and his friends. Now, if we had conclusive evidence it wasn't Eric and I *had* to pick someone for this, I'd go with John Middleton. He's the only one of my staff I could even remotely see being guilty. But that's only because for some reason he gives me a weird vibe. I watched him a lot tonight over dinner and all it did was make that vibe stronger."

He nodded. "Thanks for your input. On all of them. It truly does help, even though it's not anything that could be used to actually prosecute anyone. I hope you're right about Roberts because it's certainly less dangerous for you that way." He scrubbed his hands down his face. "Every little bit helps us figure out who did this, including gut instinct from people who've had contact with everyone involved. And on that note, I need to get some sleep so this infection doesn't kick my butt. *I* need to be the one kicking butt. Good night, Sage."

"Night."

****

The next afternoon, after shutting down her laptop for the day, Sage stood to stretch the kinks from her back and legs. She was done and it was long past time for her to be off the clock. Besides, she needed food. She picked up the stack of files she was working on and put them back in the drawer after squaring their edges.

Since there wasn't much room for file cabinets on a cruise ship, she was glad most records were kept on the computer these days.

After one last check to make sure she hadn't forgotten anything, she noticed a folded piece of notebook paper where the files had been sitting and wondered where the heck it came from. She hadn't used a notebook for years. Had one of the staff left it for her? Hopefully it wasn't important. Or worse—something that required immediate attention. An empty stomach growled imminent warnings as she picked it up

Back off.

It was written in block letters so it would be difficult to discern who might have left it. She'd not seen anyone near her private office all day, so she had no clue who could have put it there or when. Fear turned to anger.

"Back off, my ass."

Now it was personal. She wanted the culprit caught and she was going to do whatever was in her power to make that happen. Starting now. She shoved the note into the pocket of her uniform skirt and headed to John Middleton's office. Eric hadn't left the note from the grave, so he was the only one who made sense to her to be behind it all. Time to start ferreting out information in earnest.

"Hey Dr. Middleton, hope I'm not interrupting anything."

She stood in the doorway of his office, and when he looked up from working on his laptop his smile was strained. He closed the computer and motioned her to come in.

It was the end of a long day for her and, apparently,

a long one for him as well, if the fact he was still in his office was anything to go by. The staff meeting that morning seemed forever ago. At least her day was ending now, at seven o'clock, and not midnight like Dace's. She gave her head a slight shake as she sank into the visitor's chair. She wasn't going to think about Dace.

"What can I do for you?"

"I wanted to let you know how much I appreciate the support you've given me while I try to get a handle on my new position here. Though I'm only filling in at the moment and my position isn't permanent, having a new boss is always a hard transition and you've helped make it a smoother one for me. If there's anything I can do for you, just say the word."

Okay, this was going to be harder than she thought. What exactly was she supposed to say that would make him confess? This wasn't a movie where things went according to script and this wasn't a game. She stifled a sigh. She was here now, so who knows, maybe something would present itself. Running down here half-cocked wasn't one of her better ideas.

"Thanks, and please call me John when we're not on duty. I know we haven't worked together often because we previously had the same position, but we have known each other for a while now."

"Thanks. I'd love it if you'd called me Sage. Do you know if you're on the short list for the permanent position of Chief Medical Officer? Not that you have to answer that. I'm just being nosy."

She gave him a smile, the one she used to get her way. Which worked on pretty much everyone but her father. No one manipulated him. She clenched her teeth. That can of worms needed to stay locked up with the old Sage.

His smile failed to reach his eyes. "I did apply, but no one's said anything to me yet, which could mean '*no*' or could mean nothing. I think, although I've been working for the company longer, your previous experience puts you far ahead of me."

She didn't know what to say to that. She had no idea and actually no real interest, in any of it. She was just fishing for anything that might be useful to Dace. "You may be right. Is it something you'd be interested in, if they offered?"

"I think I would. It would be a nice change from caring for the crew. I know you have to be more personable because you're working with customers, so to speak."

"Yes, it is different in that aspect, and I'm enjoying the change. It's a lot of responsibility, though. More work too."

"Which translates to more money. To be honest, I'm hoping to get promoted to Chief Medical Officer eventually. However, most of the doctors they hire for the position are much older than us, with a lot more experience both in the field, as well as working on a cruise ship. Eventually I want to open my own clinic on dry land and the bigger my paycheck is now, the sooner I can do that."

"I'm considering leaving the cruise-ship life and getting a job in New Orleans, too. And you're right about some of the other doctors being better qualified. I think the only reason they offered me the job was because they needed someone who could do it right away, and as I've only got the position temporarily, who's to say where I'll end up. The fact I don't have any family ties, unlike you, may have factored in, too."

This time his smile reached his eyes. "You may be onto something there. I don't like being away from my family so much, and they may want someone who is more available. Thank you for that, Sage. I hadn't thought of it that way, and don't feel as bad about not being offered the job either temporarily or permanently. I do miss my family, but I do need to make sure it doesn't affect my work."

"That's true." She tapped her fingers on her knee, not sure what to say next. "Well, I won't keep you any longer. If you're still here, you must be trying to get caught up like I am, so I'll leave you to it." She stood up and smiled at him. "Remember, I owe you one. Don't be afraid to cash in. I'm sure the need will arise."

He laughed. "I'll hold you to it. Thanks."

She swore profusely under her breath as she walked down the hall away from his office, in search of Dace, who was theoretically on duty in the vicinity of the infirmary. She'd gleaned nothing from Middleton. The note, however, left her feeling more relieved than scared. Eric wasn't a bad guy after all, unless he could somehow leave her a note telling her to *back off,* from the grave. That little bubble of happiness popped when she remembered Dace had said something about the possibility of a partner on board who didn't have access to the pharmacy. Someone like Sean... She growled under her breath. She just wanted to know once and for all if Eric was guilty or not. She wanted, maybe even needed, him to be the man she thought he was.

Her heart thumped hard and she got all tingly when she saw Dace in the hall. Damn did he wear a security guard uniform well. He lifted his chin in greeting and picked up his pace when he saw her. "Hey Sage, done for the day?"

Then, just in case anyone saw them, he put his hands on her hips and pulled her close for a quick kiss. It shut her brain down momentarily, and she did nothing more than stare at him for a few seconds. He raised his brows, laughter lighting his eyes as he waited for her response.

She gave her head a slight shake and stepped back from him. "Yeah. I'm headed to the cabin. I'm glad I found you; there's something you need to see." She glanced around quickly and lowered her voice. "Not here. Can you come to the cabin right now?"

It turned out to be a good thing they were in her cabin when she showed him the note. "Damn it all to hell! When I catch this guy, I'm going to wring his bloody neck. And that's only the beginning. The bastard was in your office. Why don't you lock it when you're not in there?"

"There's never been a need to and it's a hassle locking and unlocking it all day while I'm working."

"So anyone on the staff could've gone in there while you were busy with a patient and left the note. Hell, a patient could've even done it. I hope they were stupid enough to leave fingerprints. Let me get an evidence bag and we'll put it in there. When we reach New Orleans, I'll have Rocque check it. On the upside, it may help us catch and convict our drug smuggler and maybe even Roberts' killer."

"Hopefully it means Eric's no longer a suspect."

He grunted. "Depends if we're looking for one person or two."

****

Less than twenty-four hours until the cruise was over. It couldn't end quick enough as far as Sage was concerned. Dace was her last patient of the morning. The staff was on lunch break, except for Celeste, but she wasn't anywhere to be found. So, Dace was in the exam room cooling his heels while she hunted up iodoform packing gauze. Which meant going to the dispensary because with the limited space on a cruise ship, it doubled as a supply closet. Ever since they'd learned someone was smuggling narcotics out of the dispensary, Sage's stomach spewed an extra shot of acid when she had to enter it. She'd be a lot happier when the ship docked in New Orleans tomorrow morning so the dreaded bottle was off the ship and in the hands of the appropriate authorities.

She wished the same could be said of Dace, but it might be a while yet before he was off her hands. She wasn't sure how long his boss wanted him playing security guard for Caribbean Seas. Even so, his arm hadn't healed enough to give him a clean bill of health. Fortunately, his white blood cell count was decreasing, which meant his body was conquering the infection. The debrided area was showing signs of healing though it was still deep enough to require the packing gauze.

She punched in the code to unlock the door. As it swung open, she wondered again what had become of Celeste. Probably grabbing some food while she had the chance. Not that Sage minded taking care of a patient by herself. Mostly she would've liked the distraction so she could focus on something other than Dace's shirtless torso while she worked on his arm.

One step over the threshold sent acid shooting

through her stomach like a water fountain. Mystery solved. Celeste was unconscious on the floor.

Chapter Thirteen

Making sure the door didn't automatically close and lock behind her like it normally did, she kicked off one shoe and used it as a doorstop. At the same time she yelled long and loud for Dace. After screaming his name, she pushed the red call button on the wall next to the door.

"*Code Alpha! Medical personnel to the dispensary STAT!*"

Not that she expected anyone to answer. The rest of the staff was on their lunch break, which meant she needed to send out the stat page via her cell phone, too. Most important was to make certain Celeste was alive. *Please God, let her be alive.*

Rushing over to her, she knelt down at her side, placed a finger on her carotid artery and prayed for a pulse. Her breath came out in a whoosh. Not only could she feel one, she saw Celeste's chest moving. As she positioned her to make a more thorough examination, she noticed a red mark on her forehead. Maybe she'd passed out and hit her head. As a diabetic, Celeste's insulin levels could be off which would explain everything. Checking her blood sugar was next on the list.

Jumping to her feet, she grabbed a glucose monitor and some oral dextrose, then sent out the emergency call on her phone. Thank God for the unified wireless network recently installed in all the Caribbean Seas ships. Quick communication for the medical staff was important, and she'd never been more grateful for it than she was now. It was not a good thing, though, that her hands were shaking so bad. A doctor needed steady hands, and if she was going to save her friend's life, she needed to pull herself together.

She was surprised by the relief she felt when Dace joined her. Which was stupid, really. This was Celeste. She should be more eager for a nurse or doctor, anyone with more medical training than a cop. He strode in the room, knelt at Celeste's side, and took her hand. "Tell me what to do."

She handed him a tube of dextrose gel. "I'm worried she's hypoglycemic. I may need you to put this in her mouth, on the inside of her cheek, so hold onto it while I check her glucose level." Sage took a deep breath as she knelt down on the other side of Celeste and pricked her finger with a lancet, touched the dot of blood to the reagent strip, then inserted it into the glucose monitor. A few seconds later, she cursed softly. "We need to get her glucose level up *now*. Administer the oral dextrose. I'll start an IV.

"On it."

Sage sprang to her feet and went to the supply cabinet, grabbed an IV start kit off the shelf. She yanked the bag open with a vicious curse under her breath. Saving someone's life went to a whole new level when it was personal.

"Give me the kit, Sage," he said with more calm than she had right now.

Her head snapped up. "What?"

"I'm a certified EMT, remember? Part of the job

requirement. I can start the IV for you."

Relief washed over her. "Sorry, I forgot. Panic moment. It's hard to think clearly when it's your best friend's life on the line."

"Get what you need and tell me what you want me to do."

Standing, she was unable to take her eyes from Celeste for a moment before she went to the fridge and took out a vial of dextrose. As she knelt back down she gritted her teeth and forced herself to forget who she was working on so she could focus on what needed to be done.

She could do it herself, had done countless times in the ER, but was grateful for Dace's strength at the moment. She opened the vial as Dace secured the IV tubing to Celeste's arm with tape and connected the tip of the syringe into the IV port.

"This stuff is thick," she said. "You need to push it hard, fast and even."

"No problem."

Nodding, Dace grasped the vial and pushed. The muscles on his forearms bunched as he applied pressure and the viscous solution entered Celeste's veins. *Damn, he was a sight to behold.* But most certainly a distraction she didn't need right now.

"What's going on, Doctor? I heard the call for help, but no one else seems to be around. Can I do anything?"

Sage glanced at the doorway before focusing on Celeste again. "Sean. What are you doing here?"

"Celeste was filling a prescription for me. I haven't had a chance to pick it up since Dr. Middleton prescribed it the other day."

With other things on her mind, she said, "Hunt up a blanket for Celeste. She's diabetic. Her blood sugar level's off and she passed out."

When he returned with the blanket, the dextrose had infused but hadn't taken effect yet. "Come on, girl," Sage begged. "Wake up for me."

"Just give her a minute," Dace warned softly. "It hasn't been that long. She'll come around."

His calm assurance helped her focus. She knew it was anxiety for her friend that made it feel like hours had passed when in reality it was mere minutes. His voice was like a soothing balm, settling her nerves.

"You're right, I know. She'll be okay."

All of a sudden, Celeste's eyelids fluttered, then her arms moved. Sage let out a breath as the truckload of pressure on her chest eased. "Hey, girlfriend, you're back." Celeste made a weak attempt to sit up but Sage put a restraining hand on her shoulder. "Stay still, you're all right. Your blood sugar dropped, and you whacked your head pretty good when you passed out from it."

"Wha—" she mumbled, glancing around. "Sean? Dr. Middleton?" She closed her eyes for a moment and licked her lips. "Dr. Middleton, where's Dr. Middleton?" Her voice rose in panic and she tried again to sit up.

Sage placed a restraining hand on her arm. "Shush. You've a ways to go yet before you can get up. I'm going to check your glucose level again. Lie quietly and let us take care of you. We'll get you in a bed in a few minutes, once I'm sure you're stable. You scared the crap out of me, girl!"

"But, Dr. Middleton…"

"Celeste, you don't need him. I can take care of you. I know I'm your friend, and not your doctor, but it doesn't matter right now. Let's just get you out of the woods first."

"Okay."

Sage let out a grateful breath when she took another blood sample, and the result was where it needed to be.

Celeste glanced groggily at Sean. "I'm guessing I wasn't able to give you your ibuprofen and that's why you're here?"

Sage chuckled and brushed the hair off Celeste's forehead. "Everyone's out to lunch. Sean and Dace were the first ones to respond when I called for help. You're still a little loopy from your blood sugar level wacking out. Don't worry. It'll all come back eventually. You didn't have a chance to fill Sean's scrip, but I can take care of it once I know you're okay."

She looked up at Sean who was behind Dace, his gaze focused on what Dace was doing, before she turned her attention back to Dace. He unscrewed the dextrose vial from the IV, discarded it, and then attached a syringe of saline to flush the IV line clear of the sticky solution.

She cleared her throat in an effort to ease its tightness. "Would one of you find a stretcher so we can move her to a bed as soon as she's stable?"

Sean spoke up. "I've worked here a while, I think I know where one is."

Celeste's eyes went wide for a moment, causing Sage to wonder if something was wrong. What she said worried her more. "Where's your shirt, Dace? Y'all playing doctor with Sage during lunch?" She giggled breathlessly. "Whoa…" Her eyes rolled and her lids fluttered down.

Thank goodness. Sage was worried what else might come out of Celeste's mouth while she was in this state, and made a mental note to be careful what secrets she shared with her from here on out.

She repeated the glucose levels and, satisfied Celeste was stable, sent out a call for the scheduled medical staff to let them know lunch time was over early. She needed someone to monitor Celeste while she finished up with Dace and took care of Sean's prescription.

Once Sean returned with the stretcher and both of the men placed Celeste on it, she ordered Sean to the waiting area, and Dace back to the exam room. Then, when she was alone, she quickly filled Sean's prescription, making double sure it was from the correct bottle, taking note of the fact the nefarious bottle was in the same spot she'd seen it last. She pocketed the prescription then grabbed the iodoform she'd come in search of, and wheeled Celeste into a treatment/observation room. She stayed with her until a nurse arrived to take her place, which fortunately wasn't too long, gave the nurse a list of instructions, and told her to call immediately if anything wasn't right. When she finally rejoined Dace in the exam room it felt like it had been a million years since she'd left him there.

"Well, back to what we were doing… Do you need a doctor's note so you don't get in trouble for being late again?" After setting the iodoform on the counter, she went to the sink and washed her hands.

"Since I was helping with a medical emergency which is part of my job description, I'm officially working. I let my boss know what happened, so technically I'm not late. We just stopped in Mexico, so you know what that means? The medical staff will be doing a few drug tests on the crew today."

A nod was her only response as she concentrated on washing her hands at the sink. It was kind of nice that drug screening wasn't part of her job anymore. She pulled on a pair of disposable gloves and got down to business. After a moment, she looked up and smiled. "Looks like you're finally on the mend, Dace. The wound edges are closing in nicely; there's no more drainage. Your fever is gone. How are you feeling? Any headaches? Fatigue? What's your pain level today?"

"No headache. The pain had lessened when I woke up this morning, but I've taken painkillers since, so I can function properly while I'm working. Slept really well last night, so I don't feel as tired. Uninterrupted sleep seems to have done the trick."

"Good. Do you think the ibuprofen is doing a better job of managing your pain?"

He shrugged a shoulder, the ripple of his muscles a distraction that had her missing the first part of his answer.

"—to be."

She'd take it as a yes since she could tell he was doing better. So she cleaned the wound, applied the iodoform and bandaged it back up in silence, feeling rather sad this was the last time she'd be taking care of him. A lump formed in her throat at the thought. She was more upset about that than she was about leaving

Caribbean Seas?

She'd known the man for five days, and merely thinking about not seeing him after tomorrow made her want to climb into her bed and curl up in a ball to ward off the pain.

She looked at his profile as he watched her hands bandage his wound. She was close enough to see the beginnings of his stubble, the smile lines around his eyes and mouth. It took all she had to keep her hands from shaking with the longing to trace those lines. To stop herself from kissing the nape of his neck, to luxuriate in the softness of his hair as she combed her fingers through it. Things she'd never had the desire to do with any other man she'd been with. She'd always focused on other, more self-satisfying aspects of the man. She was shocked to realize she'd never wanted to *caress* a man before. Her goal had always been to excite then get off. She stifled a gasp and the ache in her heart magnified.

"Everything okay, Sage? Did you find something wrong with my arm?"

Dace's words sounded a long way off, and it took a moment for her to regroup, to focus on the task at hand. She cleared her throat but the lump there refused to budge. She shook her head, and her voice came out huskier than she wanted. "You're all set. If you can get in to see your regular doctor in New Orleans in the next day or two, that would be great. Otherwise, if you're staying on the ship for another cruise, I'll give your chart to Dr. Middleton, and he can take care of you from here on out. Go ahead and put your shirt back on."

He didn't. He just sat there looking at her with those icy blue eyes that made all sorts of unwanted feelings ricochet around inside her. Whatever tomorrow brought, one thing was for certain. She had to get away from this guy. He had no idea how close he brought her to undoing everything she'd worked hard to become over the last few years. And the idea of something more deep and lasting with him scared the crap out of her right now.

"I'm not the bad guy here, Sage. And don't take your stress about Celeste out on me."

"It's not about Celeste. It's about me. We'll be in New Orleans tomorrow. I feel like we've been on this cruise for a decade, and I just want to make it home without issues of any kind."

He slid off the table and slowly picked up his shirt, fiddling with the collar but making no attempt to put it on. "Sorry to disappoint."

"What does that mean?"

He shrugged into the shirt and Sage almost let out a sigh of relief, but he didn't button it up. Instead he reached in his pants pocket and pulled out a plastic bag with a bottle in it, holding it so she could read the label. "I found this on the floor, close to where Celeste collapsed, under the base of the cupboard."

She frowned. "Humulin R. Celeste was probably trying to take a dose of insulin, collapsed before she could, and dropped the bottle."

"The bottle is empty, Sage, and there was no evidence of it having spilled. Correct me if I'm wrong, but since it's empty, that means she *would* have taken it."

Muttering something foul, she sucked her upper lip between her teeth, chewing on it as she thought things through. "Each vial of insulin contains multiple doses.

Robyn Rychards

Diabetics only take one dose at a time, depending on their sugar level." She blew out a frustrated breath and mumbled another curse. "If she'd given herself a dose, where's the syringe? Where's her insulin kit? Celeste never goes far without it."

He edged closer. "See if I'm getting this. Celeste didn't collapse because she *needed* insulin. Her glucose was low not high. That's means—"

A mixture of panic and horror took over. She reached for the doorknob, intent on going to Celeste's bedside and not leaving her alone. "Someone tried to kill my friend. That's what you're saying. Jesus, Dace, they could be with her right now trying to finish the job."

"Hey, settle down. Celeste's still pretty disoriented and hasn't been able to say one way or another what happened. While I was waiting for you to look at my arm, I called in a security guard to stay with her. It's a friend of hers, pretending to be there visiting, so if someone did try to get rid of her, they won't be suspicious and escalate things. She's safe for the moment."

Sage swallowed a lump in her throat and nodded. "If someone did try to overdose her with insulin, that rules out Sean."

He smiled indulgently. "I love the way you keep trying to eliminate suspects." Then muttered, "Though not that it's Sean."

"But he wouldn't have been able to get into the dispensary, much less know where to find insulin on the spur of moment. I'm guessing that's the case, anyway, because Sean's prescription is for ibuprofen. If someone did try to kill Celeste it was because they

212

thought she'd discovered the bottle with the hydrocodone in it. Which, by the way, it is exactly where I found it the last time I checked."

"One thing I've learned in my job, Sage, is that people you think you know, do things you would never expect. Celeste might very well have allowed Sean come with her while she filled the prescription, and if it's his bottle of narcotics, he'd know exactly where it was being stored and put it back."

"But how would he have access to the dispensary in the first place?"

"He could be working with someone on the staff or he could've stolen the security code."

Goosebumps raised on her arms at the thought. First her judgment about Dr. Roberts had been called into question. Now Celeste? Breaking the rules for the dispensary and taking Sean in there with her didn't jibe with the woman she knew.

"Yes," she acknowledged on a sigh. God, how she wished she'd never been asked to work this cruise. She'd have been much happier living in total ignorance or finding out about it all after the fact.

"Listen, I know you might be busy with patients all afternoon, but you need to find out what happened to Celeste as soon as she's coherent and remembers. It'll raise less suspicion if you do it rather than someone in an official capacity. Check in with her as often as you can and let me know what she says."

He stepped over to her, placed a hand on her cheek and using his thumb, tipped her face up. It helped settle her nerves, calmed her. It worried her that a simple touch could do that for her. Her eyes met his and tingles buzzed down her spine at the emotion smoldering there.

"I'm starting to get really pissed at this guy now. Any friend of yours is a friend of mine. It got personal with that note on your desk, and if they've done this to Celeste, then Rocque's orders be damned. When we know who's doing this, I'm taking them down." He ran his thumb along her jaw, then dropped his hand.

"You *are* starting to feel better. Until now you've been content playing security guard and stalking people."

"Amazing what ten hours in your bed will do for a guy."

She stood because looking up at him put a crick in her neck. Of course, that move put her dangerously close. And he still hadn't buttoned his shirt. "Oh, you have *no* idea, my friend. Now button up your shirt and get back to work before you get us both in trouble."

She closed the door to the exam room behind her. Having Dace all protective of her was nice, but it had its drawbacks. She had no intention of letting him know she planned on gleaning information from Sean. After giving Dace a few moments to leave the infirmary, she went to the waiting area, stopping in the doorway to scan the room. "Hey, Sean, do you mind coming to an exam room for a minute before I give you your prescription, or do you need to get back to work?"

"I have a few minutes left on my lunch break yet, so that's fine. Is there something wrong?"

"Let's talk about it in the room, okay?"

"Sure."

"Room two is fine. Second door on the right. Can you make your way there, or do you need someone to show you? I have to take care of something real quick, before I can join you."

"No problem. I can find my way."

She stood back and held the door open for him as he entered the hall. She didn't really have anything to do, but she wanted a good look at how he moved as he walked, without him knowing she was doing it. She pretended to be busy at the receptionist's desk as she watched him make his way down the hall. Once he was in the room, she waited a few minutes before joining him.

"So… Is there a problem?" he asked before she had a chance to close the door behind her.

Just in case things took a turn for the worse, she left the door slightly ajar, hoping he wouldn't notice. The rest of the staff for the afternoon shift would show up any moment; it wouldn't be long before there were too many people around for him to pull anything, were he so inclined. Something about Sean clicked in her head as she watched him help Dace get Celeste onto the stretcher. She needed to find out if she was on the right track.

"No, not a problem, per se. I pulled your chart, to check your prescription, and just wanted to discuss some things with you." She walked over to the sink, and leaned back against it, crossing her arms. "I believe it's because you sprained your wrist?"

"Yes."

"Then why aren't you wearing a brace or an ace bandage?"

He sat in a chair, rather than on the exam table, and he shifted in his seat. His eyes darted sideways before focusing on her. "I don't like wearing it when I'm on duty. I do sleep with it on, though. Stupid, I know."

"You must be in a lot of pain if you need such a

high dose of ibuprofen."

"When I'm working and not wearing a brace on my wrist, it hurts like hell. I use the ibuprofen so I can do my job without looking injured. A spotter wearing a brace does not instill confidence in someone climbing the rock wall."

It made sense. "I've known you since I first started working for Caribbean Seas, Sean, though I haven't always worked with you. I've been your doctor on several occasions. A sprained elbow, and a sprained wrist, that I remember off the top of my head, but you've been treated more times than that by a number of the ship's doctors over the years for the same type of thing."

Crossing his arms, he blew out a breath and huffed. "What are you getting at Dr. Brady? You think I'm making things up to get drugs?"

"Interesting you jumped to that conclusion. Do you mind hopping up on the exam table, I'd like to check a few things."

He shrugged. "Whatever floats your boat."

"Has the wrist been getting worse? It's been a few days now since Dr. Middleton prescribed the pain killers and you're just now getting them."

"Actually, I tweaked it again this morning, and that's why I decided to pick up the script. I was hoping to avoid another doctor's visit going in my file."

"Okay. I won't put this one in your file then. Let me have a look at it."

He held it out for her, and she took it gently in her hands, checking it for range of motion and pain, watching his face closely as she did so. He was pretty good at pretending it didn't hurt. Almost like it was a habit to hide the pain. She didn't like it. Was he hiding something? Or was he so accustomed to pain, pretending it wasn't there was second nature?

"Has the swelling changed since the initial injury?"

"No. Though I've been icing it like Dr. Middleton suggested. That's another reason I decided to start taking the meds."

"What about elevating it?"

"Mmmm… Probably not as much as I should."

"I suggest doing that as soon as you're off the clock today. And I do want you taking the ibuprofen. I'll get you a glass of water before you go so you can take it right away." She laid his arm gently on his lap. "Now, I want to have a look at your other arm." Without waiting for a response, she picked that one up, turning it so his palm faced up. She placed one hand under his elbow and wrapped her fingers around his wrist, then applied enough pressure on the elbow to check its mobility in the opposite direction it would normally go. She suppressed a smile. She loved it when she was right.

"Am I right in assuming your other elbow can bend backward too?"

"Yes."

"How about your fingers? Pretty flexible?"

"Yes."

She checked the range of motion in some of his other joints as well, a test designed to diagnose the problem she suspected he might have. A problem that occurred to her when they'd discussed his lanky frame in Belize. She was glad to have the opportunity to examine him without having to come up with a reason to get him into the infirmary for a regular appointment.

Especially since he wasn't her patient any longer.

"Do you frequently have joint pain, other than from a sprain or strain?"

He pursed his lips as he contemplated the question. "Yes, I suppose I do. Something always tends to be aching."

She sat down on a rolling stool, facing him. "I'm pretty sure you have Joint Hypermobility Syndrome. I'd like you to see your regular doctor so they can run further tests and give you an official diagnosis. With as many sprains as you've had over the course of your employment with Caribbean Seas, and the general joint pain you experience, it would be my guess that's what is going on."

"Truth, Doctor?"

"That would be nice, Sean."

"I'm not sure I want an official diagnosis. It could mess up my qualifications for this job. Other than the annoyance of the injuries, I've been coping with the other issues, and trying not to medicate whenever possible. Unless things deteriorate, is there any problem with leaving things status quo?"

This was the most frustrating part of her job. A patient who didn't want to do what was in their best interests. And she didn't believe him about not medicating. He'd purchased illegal drugs in Belize. She took a deep breath and let it out slowly. The ball was in his court, she'd done what she could, anything else was up to Sean. As much as she wanted too, she couldn't force treatment on him.

"Ultimately, your health care is your decision. I'm not real thrilled with having to turn a blind eye to this, but since you can't take all the tests needed for an official diagnosis here, I can't put it in your chart that you have the syndrome. So how you handle it is up to you for now."

He gave her a half smile. "Thanks for that. And I appreciate your concern. I *am* happy to know why I keep getting these injuries, if that makes you feel better."

"Please be careful, Sean. It seems like it's not big a deal that your joints are extra-flexible, but if you have internal muscles that do the same thing, it could be dangerous and effect the function of your organs. *Please* see a doctor about this. At the very least, research all you can on it and seek medical help if you suspect a problem. "

Sean ran a hand around the back of his neck and nodded. He met her gaze, the look in his eyes open and honest, with a hint of fear. Good. She wanted him to take it seriously. "I will, Dr. Brady. I'm not taking this lightly. Thank you for your help. I just don't want anything permanent on my record before I decide what I want to do."

"Understandable." She pulled the bottle out of her pocket and handed it to him. "For now, this should do the trick. I'll let you get back to work. I need to do the same. The receptionist can get you some water to take your meds." She stood up and he did as well. She held out her hand and he shook it. "Take care of yourself."

"I will. Thanks."

After Sean left, she was glad to have a reasonable explanation for his problems. Glad to know he wasn't manipulating things to get prescription drugs. She still didn't have a plausible reason for the drug deal they watched go down in Belize, but her instincts were screaming that Sean wasn't connected to the drugs in the dispensary or Dr. Roberts' death. If his condition was worse than he let on, it could very well be why he purchased the cocaine in Belize. To self-medicate. Though what had he done with it? Was he working with someone else on board?

She should ask Dace if he noticed anyone hanging out with Sean who could be working with him. She shook her head at herself and stood up. Dace was a professional, he'd probably already explored that angle. She smoothed down her skirt, tucked in her blouse, and headed out of the room to tackle the rest of her day.

Chapter Fourteen

It was getting late, only a few hours left on his shift, less than twelve before they reached New Orleans. Sage refused to go back to her cabin, even though Dace promised to stay with Celeste until the boat docked in the morning. The fact she didn't think it was good for his health to pull an all-nighter might have something to do with it. Or it could be because she was on call all night, and figured she'd be handy if he collapsed, or some such female silliness.

Though Celeste was holding her own, she was, as yet, unable to give them a clear picture of what happened in the dispensary. He was hoping to find out before they reached port, but the longer she slept, the less likely that became. He sighed and shifted in the molded plastic chair. Hospital rooms didn't have the most comfortable accommodations for visitors; on a cruise ship even less so. It was going to be a long night.

At the same time, he wasn't ready for the cruise to end. Amazing how things could change so drastically in less than a week. Who knew one person could change everything for you? *His* life would never be the same. Just thinking about the possibility of never seeing Sage again once they reached New Orleans left an aching pit of nothingness in his gut. He had no idea if Rocque wanted him back on duty yet, or if he was going to make him take another cruise—or five—with

Caribbean Seas.

He wrapped his hands around the back of his neck, and blew out a gusty sigh. Before Donato died he'd always faced facts. *So, you care about her Langdon, deal with it. She doesn't care about you for anything more than sex. Deal with that, too.* He dropped his hands, leaned back in the chair, and crossed his arms. He was not looking forward to a long night alone with his thoughts. He needed Celeste coherent so he could have something else to concentrate on.

"Why the big sigh?"

"Life."

"It'll do that to you. Why are you sitting here with me?"

He raised his brows and smiled slightly. "Guard duty?"

"I don't think so. I'm not in need of a security guard." She swiped her hands down her face. "Hell, maybe I am."

He perked up in his seat and uncrossed his arms. "What makes you say that? Did you remember something?"

"A little. Has anyone talked to Dr. Middleton? He knows. On second thought, maybe I should be talking with the Chief Security Officer."

"He's authorized me to hear what you have to say if you feel something suspicious happened."

"If something suspicious happened, I need to hear from the chief who I should be talking to about it. You just started working here this week, and although Sage may know you, *I* don't."

"I can't fault you for being cautious. I'll call him. Will speaking on the phone with him suffice?"

"Yes."

When she hung up the phone it took her a few moments to set it down and look at him.

"What do you remember Celeste? Dr. Middleton hasn't said much more, other than you were fine when he left the dispensary."

"Well, that's just weird. I distinctly remember him being there right before I lost consciousness. He said he would report it right away."

"Report what?"

"Sorry. Still just a tad foggy. That someone is smuggling hydrocodone in a bottle labeled ibuprofen."

"We were wondering if you found that out when you were filling Sean's prescription."

"You know? How did *you* find out?"

"Sage filled my prescription out of that bottle, and I took one thinking it was the ibuprofen. The result was not pretty."

"So you've known about it the whole time? What was it doing in the dispensary then? Though that probably explains why it wasn't where we usually store the NSAIDS."

"Because we wanted to see if we could find out who put it there and didn't want to have any problems with the smuggler while the cruise was underway." He leaned forward in his chair, placed his elbows on his knees. "Celeste, we need to know if your blood sugar level was off, and that's what almost sent you into a diabetic coma."

"My sugars were fine the last time I checked, and I wasn't feeling like anything was wrong. It was lunch time, so my glucose could have been a bit off, but I didn't notice a problem, or I wouldn't have tried to fill

Sean's prescription. I would've taken care of my blood sugar, and made him come back later. Since I'm diabetic, they don't have a problem letting me eat whether I'm working or not. It's usually pretty slow at lunch, so I was the only one there. Well, except for Dr. Middleton. I'm not sure why he was there. We didn't have any patients, and now that I think about it, he didn't say what he was doing in the dispensary."

Dace nodded and tried to keep his expression neutral so Celeste stayed calm. Though what he wanted to ask her next would most likely get her worked up. And as far as he was concerned, there was no way to put it that wouldn't irritate her. "Did you let Sean come in there with you while you filled his prescription?"

He suppressed the smile when she bristled. It was the reaction he was hoping for. For Sage's sake. For himself, he just wanted the truth regardless.

"What kind of stupid question is that? I like my job. I wouldn't do something like that to jeopardize it."

"Listen, Celeste. I'm not going to get you in trouble if you did. I just need to know. Since there was no one else around to report you if you let him tag along with you, it's easy enough to get away with."

"Well, good to know I'd be off the hook, but like I said, it was just me and Dr. Middleton. You know, it could be, since we're so close to the end of the cruise, the doctor decided it was better to wait until we docked to report the hydrocodone."

He nodded. Not that he necessarily agreed, but it was best Celeste thought so. "Could be. Nothing strange or out of the ordinary comes to mind right now though?"

She shook her head, and shifted in an effort to get

more comfortable, which made her wince and suck in a breath. "My hip hurts like hell. I wonder if I hurt it when I fell. Damn. It feels like I've been given a tetanus shot in my butt."

Hell. Not good. "Sage is working the night shift. Want me to go get her so she can have a look?"

"Might as well, I guess. Give us all something to do."

"Okay. I'll be right back."

****

Sage decided to check on Celeste, and though she tried to convince herself it had nothing to do with Dace being in there, it didn't work. She wanted to take advantage of the opportunity to see him because very soon the opportunity would no longer exist.

Sitting alone in her office for the last several hours gave her the time to process everything that had happened in the last week. The soul-searching brought some inner peace. She knew her decision to resign from Caribbean Seas was a good one. Even if it meant she'd be living in the same city as Dace, the odds of running into him in a place the size of New Orleans weren't that great. Which left her feeling…awful. Which was new. Even when she'd been in a committed relationship, and contemplating making it permanent, she never panicked at the idea of never seeing the guy again. The mere thought of never seeing Dace after tomorrow had her feeling like she was coming down with the flu. Achy inside and out.

God. She stopped in the middle of the corridor. Could she be experiencing all these strange sensations because she was in love with the man? In less than a week? Did that actually happen to people? She'd been in lust before, been so hot for a man she had a hard time concentrating on anything else, but this thing she had for Dace was not that. Oh, she lusted after him in the same way, but what she felt now was so much more than anything she'd felt before, every other man paled in comparison.

She shook her head in denial and started walking again. She should stop at the dispensary to grab some insulin for Celeste. By now the entire staff was aware of what happened, but Dace still didn't know if it had been a deliberate attempt on her life or not. Therefore, though she'd normally have a nurse assigned to take care of her, she wasn't taking any chances. She punched in the code, pushed open the door, and stopped in her tracks when she saw Dr. Middleton inside with *the* bottle of ibuprofen in his hand, the black dot on the bottom clear for her to see. Now her stomach issues had nothing to do with the flu. Her gut was screaming, *he's the guy*. Why else was he in here, at this time of night when *she* was the on-call doctor? He wasn't in uniform, and he had a laptop bag over his shoulder. On top of which, he'd dug that bottle out of the back of the cabinet.

She ground her teeth as her temper started to rise, positive he was the son of a bitch who'd killed Dr. Roberts, and probably had tried to kill Celeste. He slipped the bottle in his bag, still unaware he had an observer. The door slipped out of her hand and slammed shut. He swung around to face her, an expression of shocked horror crossing his face before it was quickly replaced by a pleasant smile.

The last thing she wanted to do was confront him by herself, locked in the dispensary late at night, so she decided to pretend she hadn't seen him take the bottle and pray someone could catch him with it later. "Hello, John. I need to grab some insulin for Celeste before I check on her. What brings you here this time of night?"

Damn. Should she have asked him that? She was putting him on the spot, and it wasn't a good idea to make him nervous. Still, it seemed like something anyone would ask considering the circumstances.

He leaned back against the counter and crossed his arms. Trying to appear nonchalant? His eyes shifted sideways before coming to rest on her face. "I ran into Sean at the crew member's bar, and he asked me for the prescription he didn't pick up the other day. I guess his wrist is still bothering him. I already returned the pills to the bottle, but I told him I could refill it and bring it to him. How's Celeste doing?"

"She's been rather out of it since the episode, but no longer in danger."

She walked over to the fridge, covertly keeping an eye on him as she did. "You know, Celeste said she was filling Sean's prescription, that's why she was in the dispensary when she collapsed. She also said you were there with her."

What a stupid thing to say.

She quickly grabbed the vial of insulin, closed the refrigerator, and turned to face him. That was the problem with saying the first thing that popped in your head. Things came out of your mouth better kept to yourself. If she let on she knew what he was up to, she was screwed. Celeste hadn't actually told her he'd been there, but the fact she'd asked for Dr. Middleton made Sage think he was, and seeing him pilfering that bottle, she was pretty sure that was the case. She'd bet her life he'd overdosed Celeste on insulin. Hell, she *was* betting her life. She suppressed a shiver and tried not to think about it. Now definitely wasn't the time. She might be cool, calm and collected in a medical emergency, able to think quickly and make good decisions, but this sort of life or death situation with people she cared about, never mind herself, had her making some pretty stupid moves.

He stepped away from the counter toward her, and when she looked in his eyes, her heart started clamoring in her chest. *Jesus.* The man was high as a kite. Cold fear crept down her spine. His hands were behind his back. Was he up to something? She just stopped herself from shaking her head at herself. She was being paranoid.

"What else did she say? Did she tell you what she found?"

Did he realize he'd given himself away? Not that she was going to let him know she'd realized it. Why couldn't she have just kept her mouth shut? She shrugged and slowly made her way to the door. She was closer to it than he was, and it gave her a sense of security. The intercom was next to the door too, so it was an option if things suddenly turned ugly. She also had her phone she could use to call for help.

Trying to appear careless, Sage shrugged. "It was hard making sense of some of what she said, actually. She was pretty clear though, about you being with her. Did she tell you she found something? She didn't say anything about that."

He shook his head. "I was here when she came in, but she seemed fine, and as I was finished with what I came for, we just greeted each other and I left."

If he was going to ignore his statement about finding something, she was too. It wouldn't do her any good for him to know she knew about the bottle. Her panic subsided when she reached the door, and she put her hand behind her on the knob while she faced him. She sure wasn't going to turn her back on the guy, not even while she was leaving.

Suddenly the urge to call him on everything overwhelmed her. Dace was just down the hall with Celeste, the intercom was right next to her, her hand was on the door knob. And she knew Judo. A surge of adrenaline pumped through her, and the desire to let him know he wasn't going to get away with any of it flooded her, confident she could get away from him if he grabbed her. This man had hurt people she cared about and he had to pay. She wanted a full confession so there wasn't some kind of loophole allowing him to get away with killing one friend, and almost killing another.

"Did she tell you what she found, John? Was it per chance that bottle you put in your bag?"

She cursed herself when she saw the look on his face. She cursed the adrenaline junkie in her, as well as her overwhelming desire to defend and protect the people she cared for. She should've left when she had the chance. Lightening quick, he stepped closer and trapped her between himself and the door. A door that opened inward and therefore made it virtually impossible for her to open since they were so close to it.

"How long have you known, Sage?"

She needed a new plan. Maybe if she distracted him by going for the intercom, then disabled him with a well-aimed kick. Before she could do more than make a move in that direction, he grabbed her, spun her around to face the door, and yanked her arm up behind her back. She kicked her foot backward in an attempt to hurt him where it counted, hard enough to make him see stars for a week, but his other arm snaked around her waist before she could complete the action, pinning her free arm against her side. He pulled her tightly back against him, giving the arm he held behind her back a vicious tug, just hard enough to make her think he was going to break it. Trapping it in position between his body and hers, he let go of it.

It wasn't until the pain in her arm subsided that she noticed the scalpel in his other hand. She tried to struggle loose, to butt her head up and hit him in the chin, but the hold on her waist tightened to the point she could hardly breathe, increasing the pain in the arm behind her back. The world began to spin, and all she could concentrate on was getting enough air. She couldn't pass out, her life depended on remaining conscious.

He transferred the scalpel to his free hand and held it to her carotid. She instantly stilled. If he cut her there, if she moved too much and the knife sliced her merely because of its proximity, she could bleed out faster than anyone could find her. She had to stop reacting and *think*. Maybe if she got him talking it would buy enough time for someone to come along and see what was going on. They were right in front of the window on the door, for god's sake. All it would take was someone walking down the hall. She wasn't going to think about the fact they were locked in. Or that it was the middle of the night, and hardly anyone was around. *Dace* was around. So, one problem at a time.

It wasn't a good idea to let him know how long she'd known about the drug smuggling, or that she wasn't the only one who knew, but getting him talking was definitely in her favor. She took a slow deep breath, careful not to move her neck against the scalpel. A blade designed to cut flesh.

"I haven't known about it long. But why, John? I find it hard to fathom a doctor who's spent so much time learning to help people, would feel money is more important than lives."

"Money makes the world go round, my dear, how could you not know that? And in my world, I need a lot of it. My daughter was premature, the bills from that were astronomical, much less the ongoing health care she needs, I have student loans to repay, my wife has expensive tastes. Do you have any idea the kind of financial stress I've been under? And then they give *you* the job of Chief Medical Officer? I'm the one who deserved it. I've been here longer than you, and I need the money more than you."

Holy crap! There wasn't much she could do to talk him into sparing her life if that's where he was coming from. Now what? *Slow, deep breath. Sympathize. Distract. Just buy some time.*

Quietly, in the most soothing voice she could muster, she said, "I don't blame you, John. Every man wants to take care of his family. Give them everything they want. I can't imagine how heartbreaking it was for you with your daughter, wondering if she was going to live. All the extra care a premature baby needs when they get home. I bet it even made you feel trapped in this job because you couldn't afford the insecurity of starting something new."

It wasn't much, but she felt his hold relax a little. Not enough for her to free herself, but enough that the scalpel eased away from her neck so it didn't feel on the verge of cutting her open every time she took a breath.

"Yes. That's right. I need this job, I need to take the drugs to cope, and I need the income from selling them. Now, I need you gone so I can keep doing what I've been doing. I also need the promotion. Without you around to turn the Captain's head by sleeping with him, by how pretty you are, I can be the Chief Medical Officer like I deserve to be."

"I only took the job temporarily, John. I'm not going to take it if they offer it to me permanently. I'm quitting Caribbean Seas. It's still available, and with you already on board and willing to do the job, I'm sure they'll offer it to you."

"They better. Though I want you to know, I didn't kill Roberts for his job. He just stumbled across the pills, like you. Like Celeste. So I had no choice. I tried to make it look like they died of natural causes. Which worked with Eric, and almost worked with Celeste. I'm going to have to fix that now and do something to make it look like you weren't murdered either. Suicide maybe?"

"I'm glad you didn't kill him hoping to get his job. I really do understand you needed to do everything in order to get the money to take care of your family. You did what you had to do, John. I get it."

She felt him relax some more. So far, so good. But what more was there to say? Keeping him talking until someone came along to help her was fast becoming unrealistic. She had to think of something else, preferably before he figured out how to kill her so it looked like suicide. He'd eased his hold, and he had to be getting tired. Maybe it was time to try a judo move.

"I'm glad you understand. I'm not a bad person. I'm just doing what I need to do to take care of the people who are important to me."

"I do see that. A good father and husband does whatever he has to, to take care of his family. You had no choice when you killed Eric. But you do have a choice now. You don't have to kill anyone else, John. It's not like I'm going to be working for Caribbean Seas anymore. I can just leave, and never say a word to anyone. As for Celeste, well, she can work with you. Actually, we've talked about doing it ourselves, how easy it would be, but I was too chicken. I bet she'd be willing to join your operation. With both of you doing it, you could transport more narcotics and also cover for each other. It could be a great set up."

His arm tightened around her waist, once again making it difficult for her to breathe, and he laughed sarcastically. "You really think I'm that stupid? All you're trying to do is save your life. How can you know what Celeste is willing to do? How do I know you won't go running to the cops with this the minute you get a chance?"

Her eyes stung, the back of her throat burned, and the arm he had trapped between them was numb. Hopelessness set in, and all she could think about was how stupid she was to keep Dace at arm's length. She could've had the fling of her life.

****

Dace bit back the curse he wanted to howl at the top of his lungs and flattened himself against the wall next to the door of the dispensary. He squeezed his eyes shut, but the picture of Sage with a scalpel poised on her jugular danced behind his eyelids. Right next to the one of Donato in the same position. How could this be happening again? And what were the odds things would go down the same way they had with Donato? If he had anything to do with it, zero. Sage was *not* going to die today. Even if it meant he had to.

His heart thundered in his chest, reverberating through his ears and making it hard to concentrate. What he wanted to do was storm into the room, guns blazing, and take the guy down. Not really a plausible plan, since he didn't have the access code to get in there. Or a gun. Never mind the fact they were so close to the door, Middleton would see him through the window before he had a chance to do anything. Even if he had the code, would he be able to get the door open with them standing there? The asshole was on the verge of slitting her throat, how much time did he really have to do anything? The bastard could cut her at any moment and her life would seep away in a flash. He knew. He'd watched it happen to Donato.

He tipped his head back and looked at the ceiling. *Think.*

He was a cop, his job required him to think on his feet in situations like this. Most situations didn't include Sage's life being on the line, and him wanting to die right along with her. *No one was going to die today.* He was going to get her out of there and after that, he was going to make sure he did everything in his power to convince her to stay with him for the rest of their lives. They deserved a chance to be together. That's all he wanted. A chance.

His vision cleared. His brain computed what he was looking at. Now *that* might work…

The first thing he needed to do was call for back up. He also needed to let Sage know he was there. But how? If Middleton had one whiff of being caught, all it would take is a flick of his wrist and Sage was done for. Should he risk another look inside the dispensary? *Not yet.* He moved back down the hall, away from the door, pulled out his phone and alerted security about the situation. Now, to set off the sprinkler system. Hopefully it would be enough of a distraction Sage could use her judo and get away.

He moved closer to the dispensary and positioned himself so he had a good a view through the window on the door without making it obvious he was there. He closed his eyes briefly, and his heart dropped to his shoes when he opened them and didn't see either of them. What he wouldn't give for one more chance to be with Sage. An opportunity to tell her how special she was to him. How much he loved her.

Jesus. Of all the inopportune times to realize that…

He ignored his feelings and stiffened his spine as he crept closer to the door, trying to get a better view without exposing himself any more than necessary. *Please let her be okay.* His heart hammered in his chest like a freight train and threatened to come tearing out at top speed. That was okay. It meant his adrenaline was flowing. It would come in handy any moment now.

Thank God. They'd merely moved away from the door a little bit, though they were both still facing it. Was Middleton trying to make sure no one else saw them? Then he caught Sage's eye, and peace enveloped him like a warm, comforting blanket. She wasn't giving in to fear or Middleton. She was biding her time until an opportunity to escape presented itself. And by god, he was going to give her that opportunity.

He quickly backed out of sight before the doctor noticed him and flicked on his lighter. Stepping under the nearest sprinkler head, he held the flame as close as he could, and the damn thing couldn't come on fast enough, as far as he was concerned. When it finally did, the muscles in his jaw relaxed, but the tightness in his chest didn't ease. They weren't out of the woods yet.

It was by far the best moment of his life when Sage came flying out the door into his arms, and one of his biggest let-downs when she pulled out of them right away.

"He's going to be hot on my heels Dace. I didn't incapacitate him, just took him by surprise. I like the look of you all wet, by the way."

Damn, but he loved this woman.

Chapter Fifteen

She thought the first month after leaving Chicago to work on a cruise ship was the hardest month of her life, but she was wrong. The last couple months on land beat that one by miles. Though it might have something to do with the fact she didn't do well with change, the truth was, it had less to do with change and more to do with Dace Langdon.

Not that starting a new job working at a clinic wasn't hard. There were a lot of new things to get used to, and new people to get to know. Still, the upside was well worth the angst. Aside from the satisfaction of being able to help people who really needed it, she was happy Celeste decided to join her to work as her nurse. And she'd proved to be a real emotional support as well, helping her get through the worst of it both in her personal life and her secular life.

The emotional insight Celeste had given her to help her sort her feelings, not only about Dace, but about her father, proved invaluable. Why hadn't she tapped into that long ago? She'd have been a lot better equipped to handle the whole Dace situation when it came along if she had. Water under the bridge at this point. At least she had the help she needed to view things from the proper perspective now. She could never repay Celeste for all she'd done for her, that was for sure.

But Dace... Since when had one person meant so

much to her? Not since… Well, right before she left her job in Chicago, when she finally faced reality and realized, no matter how good a doctor she was, she'd never make her father happy. It made turning him in for his drug theft the best—and hardest—thing she'd ever done. And the promise she made to herself after that, to never care about anyone so much, ever again, because in the end they let you down? Yeah, that was broken now. *Thanks Dace.*

As difficult as it was every day to drag herself out of bed in the morning and function, loving the man had taught her something about herself she was glad to know. She was capable of wanting a man for more than how good he could make her feel physically, or how well he could make her forget the world for a while. When she ached to be with him, it wasn't for what his kisses did to her. It was for his companionship. His smile. The sound of his deep voice. The laughter in his eyes. His strength. His ability to lift her mood merely by walking in the room.

What was it about *her,* that the men in her life couldn't love her the same way? She'd tried so hard to earn her father's love, and nothing she'd done was enough. Because of that, there was no way she was going to go chasing after Dace, even though her first instinct was to do exactly that. To do everything in her power to *make* him love her. Truthfully, she didn't really want someone she had to work so hard to get. It didn't get you what you wanted in the end anyway, because it wasn't real.

She couldn't blame him for making her feel like this, either. He hadn't set out to make her love him. She just had. *Because he was awesome.* How could she help but fall in love with such a man? When she feared Middleton was going to kill her and she'd never be able to see Dace again, talk to him, take care of him, touch him, or merely be in his orbit, she'd realized the depth of her feelings.

She'd also come to appreciate something else in all her soul-searching since quitting Caribbean Seas. Using sex as a way to cope with the stress of her job wasn't what she'd been doing at all. She'd actually been acting on a subconscious need to be a terrible person, because that would make it okay that her father didn't love her. And it wouldn't surprise her if loving Dace was some kind of cosmic payback for all those men she'd used. Even though she hadn't intentionally set out to use them. Water under the bridge now, though, and the only thing she could do at this point was not ever be like that again.

The decisive knock on her door made her jump. Not only did she not know anyone well enough yet that they'd stop by for a visit, she was still a little twitchy from having a scalpel pressed against her neck. She shook her head at herself as she went to answer the door. How long was that night in the dispensary going to haunt her?

She felt the color drain from her face as she grabbed the door knob in a death grip. She sucked in a deep breath. She wasn't so bad off she was hallucinating now, was she? "Dace… What are you doing here?"

"Can I come in?"

"Yeah. Sure."

Her world settled back to normal, and the sheer joy of seeing him again flooded her. She opened the door all the way so he could come in and escorted him into the living room. He'd sought her out. That had to be a good sign.

As he followed hot on her heels, she couldn't help it, she looked over her shoulder at him with a smile and a lift of her brow. "Enjoying the view?"

"Always."

She stopped when she reached the middle of the room and turned to face him. "What brings you here?"

"Unfinished business."

He shoved his hands in the pockets of his jeans, drawing her attention to things she really didn't need to be paying attention to right now. Desperate to distract herself, and afraid of what his comment might mean, she ignored it and asked something else. "Are you back to being a detective for the NOPD?"

"Back to my regular job. Had to wait for my doctor to clear me for full duty because of my injury, but I'm all healed now."

He flexed his arm for her with a smile and moved closer, though not close enough she could reach out and touch him. Still, it made her feel like backing away and pressing herself against the wall. Mostly because she didn't trust herself to keep her hands to herself if he came within touching distance, and how embarrassing would that be?

She shook her head at herself. He didn't have to do much more than be in the same room for her thinking to get all muddled. "Forgive me for being rude. Please, have a seat. Can I get you anything to drink?"

His only answer was to shake his head. She gave him a puzzled look, wondering why he was here. "How about you? What are you doing now you're not cruising for a living?"

She laughed. "You make it sound so glamorous when you know very well it's not. I'm working at a clinic for low-income people. I really wanted to do something that will make a difference in peoples' lives. I had a taste of it working in an ER, but after that last week on the ship, I decided I didn't need that kind of stress again."

He nodded, and the look in his eyes as they leisurely ran over her from head to toe and back up again, had her fighting an overwhelming urge to wrap herself around him and never let go. Then he moved closer. Close enough he was in her personal space. And the look in his eyes... Her thinking capacity plummeted, and she had a hard time focusing on anything other than what that look was doing to her.

"I'd be happy to help relieve your stress any time you need it, if you want to give the ER thing a shot again."

She shivered and suppressed a groan at the mere thought of coming home to him after a stressful day of emergency medicine and getting lost in all sorts of decadent behavior. "You have no idea how tempting that is."

Her words were enough to have him closing what was left of the distance between them to take her in his arms. "Then I'm yours. Do with me what you will."

She ran her hands up over his pecs, relishing the feel of it, memorizing the sensations, then rested them on his shoulders for a moment before twining her hands around his neck. She pressed herself against him and looked him in the eye. "I could never use you like that Dace, even at my worst."

Something flared in his eyes, and his face became serious. "Don't mess with me Sage."

She kissed him tenderly, reverently. The hands resting lightly on her hips tightened their grip, and for a moment she thought he was going to pull her closer. Her heart sank when he didn't, though he didn't let her go either. He rested his forehead against hers and closed his eyes.

"Sage, when I saw you with that scalpel at your throat, I—" He swallowed convulsively. "I realized how important you are to me. I'm not ready to say goodbye to you, and now that I have all my ducks in a row, in my job and my life…" His voice petered away, and he swallowed so hard she could hear it. He opened his eyes and pulled back from her to look at her face. "No pressure. Ignore that if you want. I just couldn't leave things with you the way they were. Also… I thought you'd want to know about Sean. You like him, and I didn't want you thinking the wrong things about him. Also, there was that note you got."

"Sean? What do you mean?"

"You can't have forgotten we took pictures of him doing a drug deal in Belize."

"Oh good grief." She shook her head at herself. Belize felt like a million years ago. "What's going to happen with that?"

"Nothing."

"Nothing? Why the hell nothing?"

Not that she didn't like Sean or wished trouble on him, but he shouldn't be getting away with smuggling drugs, dealing drugs or whatever the heck it was he was up to.

"Since neither of us are working on the ship

anymore, I can tell you what was going on, though keep in mind, this is something you can't talk about. *With anyone*. Think of it as doctor/patient privilege. No one else can know about this."

Whoa. With that kind of codicil, it had to be something big. What in the world was going on with Sean? Alarmed, she looked in Dace's eyes, which was enough to calm her down. He was serious, but not worried. That was a good sign, right? It was bad enough thinking a person she thought was a good guy could be involved in something like drug smuggling, even if it had nothing to do with what had been going on on board the ship, or Eric's murder.

"He's working undercover for the DEA. They're trying to get a handle on the drug trafficking through Belize."

Her muscles relaxed in relief. He was one of the good guys. Her initial read on him was right. It also explained why he didn't want an official diagnosis for his disease. "Well, my respect for Sean just went up several notches."

Dace grimaced but nodded. "As for the note you got, the one telling you to back off…"

She nodded. "I remember. Were you able to use it as evidence?"

He shook his head. "Middleton didn't leave it on your desk. It wasn't from him. The fingerprints on it matched my ex, Tina. Looks like I dodged a bullet not getting serious with her."

"Do you mean she was trying to stake her territory with you? That she didn't want me stealing her boyfriend?"

"Yep. Crazy."

"Did she get in trouble for the note? Or do I need to press harassment charges or something for that to happen?"

He caressed her hips with his hands and his eyes crinkled as he smiled briefly. "Don't worry about it. I put the fear of the law into her and made it very clear I'm not interested. She won't be messing with you anymore."

"I hope you didn't do anything you shouldn't have."

"Nah. It's all good now. Tina is out of the picture. However, there's something else I wanted you to know, *chère*."

He paused and looked in her eyes for several long moments before letting out a groan and capturing her lips with his. It was a kiss unlike any he'd given her, vacillating between savage and reverential. It made her eyes burn and her heart stutter. So much emotion. From him. From her. She didn't know what to do with it all. They were both breathing hard when he lifted his head. After taking one last deep breath through his nose, he continued as though he hadn't kissed her at all. Maybe he didn't know what to do with all the intensity either.

"Saving you that night helped me save myself, Sage. Seeing you in trouble like that, was a million times harder than when Donato was held at knife-point. I was so freaked out after he died, and afraid I'd freeze up the next time I was in a situation like that, or that I'd ignore my gut again, or be unsure about what to do. Basically it felt like every bit of police training I had no longer existed."

He let go of her and took a step back, and as much as she wanted to tighten her grip around his neck, she let him go. He shoved his hands in his pockets again and his eyes raked her face, his expression rather grim.

"That night Donato died… I let my emotions affect my decisions, and tried negotiating with the bad guys, simply because I didn't want things to get ugly in front of a child. Witnessing something like that can stay with you all your life, and I didn't want Donato to have a memory like that. Which meant my priorities were seriously screwed up. I was so concerned about minimizing his trauma, I wasn't focused on doing what I knew needed to be done, which was to take out those scum bags any way I could. As a result, I lost trust in myself, and in my ability to do my job. Not that I admitted it to myself until after we docked in New Orleans. That last night on the ship was an eye-opener for me."

"As soon as I saw you outside the dispensary, Dace, I knew everything was going to be okay. I guess I trusted you more than you trusted yourself."

"I'm glad the trust wasn't misplaced like Donato's was."

"Don't. Don't do that to yourself. You didn't screw up Dace. You think I don't know what it's like to have someone die on you in an emergency situation? To second-guess all your decisions for weeks afterward? It's hell, but you can't let it stop you from doing your job. From putting yourself out there again and helping other people. And trust me, I know all about quitting your job and taking the easy way out. I've spent years doing that before I woke up and got my act together. It's taken you, what, a month?"

His smile lit his eyes and he bobbed his head once in agreement. "About that… However, when you put it that way, it makes *you* look pretty bad, and from where I'm standing, that isn't the case at all. You saved yourself that night, just as much as I did. I merely kept my head together and provided a distraction."

"Knowing you had my back gave me confidence, Dace. I never doubted your ability to handle things. Besides, I don't like letting bullies have their way. It's a bit of a pet peeve with me."

"Hmmm… Something else we have in common." His voice lowered and rumbled in his chest when he added, "We'd be good together, Sage."

She tucked her hair behind her ears, then turned her back on him, wrapping her arms around her middle in an effort to suppress the feelings threatening to erupt. She couldn't look at him and think straight after a statement like that.

"I knew that the minute I saw you in the captain's quarters."

"Then don't fight this anymore, sweetheart. Give this thing between us a chance. See what it leads to."

Her breath caught, and she spun around to face him. He thought it might lead to something? Hope flared, then sputtered and died. Men didn't want her for that. They may pretend to like her for a time, like she had them, but really, previous experience taught her men didn't have deep, genuine feelings for her. Which was tragic, really, because she'd discovered she wanted a man to have those feelings for her more than she wanted air. But not just *a* man, Dace.

"Like I told you before, I'm not getting caught up in that kind of life anymore. I left Chicago to get away from it. I want to build a different life here. One that means something."

"Maybe, in order to do that, you need to stop focusing on all the things you did wrong in Chicago and look at all the things you did right. Off the top of your head, can you tell me how many people you were unable to help the whole time you worked there?"

"You mean, like how many people died because I couldn't save them?"

"Yes, but also how many people you weren't able to diagnose. I don't need you to tell me a number, but can you think of one or come up with a close guess?"

"Yes, sure, I remember every single one." She said it slowly, unsure what his point was.

He nodded as though that was the answer he expected. "Now, do you know how many people you *did* help?"

She tipped her head back and closed her eyes for a moment. "I don't have a clue." She dropped her chin and looked at him again. "I've been looking at it wrong, haven't I?"

He smiled and she wished she could have him smile at her like that every day for the rest of her life. "If it makes you feel any better, I was doing the same thing for a while. Stop letting your failures dictate your life."

He was *so* right. How could she have been so blind? And she was going to compound her stupidity by letting this man get away? No way was another failure going to dictate her actions, and failing to tell him how she felt about him because she was afraid she was unlovable, would be exactly that. "My God, Dace... I love you so much, and I can't bear to watch you walk out of my life."

He went still as a statue at her words, and she

prepared herself for the fallout from her statement. But she wasn't going to regret it. She had let him know how she felt, and she would never have to look back and wonder, *what if?*

"Sage." He breathed her name like he had when they first met, savoring the feel of it on his tongue. Before she could blink twice, she was in his arms and wondering if she was dreaming. "I love you too. In fact I'm finding it hard to believe you actually feel the same way."

She laughed breathlessly. "I know exactly what you mean. Is this really happening? Half an hour ago I was trying to figure out how I was going to survive without ever seeing you again."

"Well, if it isn't real, then I sure as hell better not wake up."

He squeezed her hard and she squeezed him right back, deciding it might work like a pinch does, to check if you're awake or dreaming. "With a hug like this, we have to be awake."

He chuckled and she put her hands behind his head, pulled it down and started kissing him all over his face, to the point he started chuckling again. "Okay, okay. I believe it. We're not dreaming. You really love me. Are you going to prove it by marrying me?"

Stunned, his words the last thing she expected to hear, she couldn't think of a thing to say. He actually wanted more than merely exploring the depth of their feelings. His intentions were honorable. Then again, the man she knew *was* honorable, as well as everything else you'd expect from someone who'd vowed to protect and serve. She couldn't do anything more than breathe, "Dace…"

Before she could gather her wits, much less answer his question, he pulled her in his arms, pressing her tightly against his length, as though by doing so he could meld them together into one entity. "You don't have to answer that yet. Just think about it while I do this."

He captured her mouth with his, stroking her lips in the most spine-tingling way. Then he caressed them with his tongue before nibbling on them lightly with his teeth, while his hands did some caressing of their own along her back. One hand tangled in her hair to cradle her head, while the other traveled slowly down her spine. He pressed it into the small of her back, locking her hips against his, making her long for him to press himself into her in a much more intimate and satisfying way.

The fire inside her that ignited whenever he walked in the room, became an inferno. She opened her mouth and deepened the kiss, at the same time pushing her hands under his shirt, desperate for skin on skin contact.

When he tore his mouth from hers, she whimpered in protest, but the momentary fear that he was stopping what they were doing vanished when he pulled off his shirt, then reached for the hem of hers, lifted it over her head and gathered her back in his arms. He rubbed himself against her, and the groan that rumbled through him was echoed by one of her own. The glorious torso she'd ached to feel so often she'd lost count, was pressed against her in the most delicious way, and it was more heavenly than she'd imagined. The feel of his hair roughened skin against the softness of hers almost more than she could bear. When he let her go to hold her at arm's length she wanted to cry.

"I need to see you, Sage. As good as you feel, I need to look at you. I've imagined it for so long…" His voice caught and he swallowed hard. His hands came to rest on her waist before moving across her stomach and up to the bare flesh exposed by her bra.

"So beautiful," he murmured. "Better than I ever imagined."

Goosebumps raised on her skin at the nearly-unbearable sensations aroused by the touch of his hands on places he'd never touched before. The intensity of it, the uniqueness of what *his* hands could make her feel, brought tears to her eyes. She quickly blinked them away for fear he'd stop if he saw them.

The honk of a car horn brought them back to reality, though not enough for Dace to take his hands from her body, just enough for them to pause on her shoulders.

"Dace…"

"My God, Sage, please don't tell me to stop. There's no good reason on earth for us to deny ourselves this."

"At this point, I don't think I could bring myself to do that even if I wanted to." She let out a breathless laugh. "I'm just thinking it might be a good idea to dial it down a bit. I don't want Celeste walking in to find us making love on the living room floor, and she should be here any minute."

He gathered their shirts up off the floor and helped her back into hers before he pulled his on. Then he chuckled and picked her up in his arms. "You know how many times I wanted to do this and my stupid injury wouldn't let me?"

"I doubt it's more than how many times I wanted

you to."

He walked over to the couch and sat down, settling her on his lap so they were both comfortable. "How's this? Presentable enough for you?"

She nodded and giggled. Celeste was going to die when she walked in on them making out on the couch.

"Now, let me show you exactly how marrying me is the best decision you'll ever make."

"I think you've already done that, but just to be sure, let the convincing commence."

A word about the author...

Robyn Rychards grew up in the granola bowl of the United States, Boulder, Colorado, a town filled with fruits, flakes, and nuts. She considers herself a Jack-of-all-trades-master-of-none and has taught herself to sew, paint, play the piano, garden, cook, the list goes on. But now that her books are published, she's thrilled to finally be considered a master of one. At least as much as a person can be, for the learning never really stops.

She feels her active imagination is a blessing and a curse, with the blessing far outweighing the curse since it has led her to fulfill her dream of being a published romance author. Robyn started writing when she was a teenager because she didn't have enough books to read, and sometimes finds it hard to believe people are willing to pay her to do something she enjoys so much. Then there's the added bonus of having a good reason to put off cooking and cleaning, much less a job that means you can stay in your jammies as long as you want. That's priceless.

http://www.robynrychards.com